DARKLY FLOWS THE TAFF

Simon - I do hope you can see this from your star!

DARKLY FLOWS THE TAFF
by Simon Barnes

Copyright (c) 2015 Jaqueline Barnes.

All rights reserved
No part of this publication may be reproduced, stored in a retrieval system, or transmitted in any form or by any means, electronic, mechanical, photocopying, recording or otherwise, without the prior permission of the copyright owner.

All characters in this publication are fictitious and any resemblance to real persons, living or dead is purely coincidental.

Acknowledgements.

Jacky Barnes would like to thank Robert Barnes and Thomas Koeller, for their technical help in preparing Simon's book for publication, and for their enormous patience in advising me.

Cover illustrations.

Front cover - from a painting 'The Cherry Tree' by Simon Barnes
Back cover - Llandovery Theatre Company production photo -
Simon Barnes as the Prime Minister in Who'll Feed the Horses'
Festival 1976.
Settings and graphic Natalie Poulson

Simon Barnes, *actor, playwright, artist and theatre director, built first his own house, and then a theatre in Wales - Llandovery Theatre - which he ran for 30 years with his actress wife Jaqueline Harrison, performing and directing Festivals, and writing over 20 plays for the Company. His career included varied performance work, from classical theatre to commercials for chicken rissoles and rice pudding, TV, stage, and film - and early struggles included working as a life guard at Hampstead Ponds, driving for the PDSA, tractor driving for Bromley Council, and at the start of his career, sleeping rough while training at the Actors' Workshop in London. This last providing rich material for his comedy play COME IN GOD - MY TIME IS UP - which was the opening production at Llandovery Theatre in 1978.*

Darkly flows the Taff, *set in 1986 - is his first and last novel.*

Darkly flows the Taff by Simon Barnes

Foreword by Horatio Nelson

I thoroughly recommend this book as a good read. I am particularly impressed as Mr Barnes has a cat featured in it - albeit only briefly - but it is a significant contribution. So many modern writers ignore the feline species in their novels, such a mistake, I think.

Had I, of course, seen the script in embryo, I would have suggested incorporating a cat in the scenes where the unfortunate hero, Rupert, is stuck up a tree! A feline companion and adviser on how to stay up, and possibly even get down from said tree, would have been of great value to the story, not to mention the hero!!

This book is such fun and so well written, though perhaps I should acknowledge a slight bias in the author's favour, as Mr Barnes was instrumental in saving several of my nine lives!

Horatio Nelson - Theatre Cat
Thoughts from my window-sill!

DARKLY FLOWS THE TAFF
by Simon Barnes

Contents

1	England Expects	1
2	Across Offa's Dyke.	13
3	Far Flung out-posts of the Empire	28
4	In Need of Slight Renovation Sir…	42
5	Home on the range	52
6	It's a Man's Life	60
7	Beware the Gifts Bearing Leeks	68
8	Arts and Grafts	80
9	Reflections in Iced Cold Lager	103
10	Some Men of Harlech	108
11	Of Champagne, Leeks and Death	120
12	A touch of the Megans in the Night	134
13	Take it easy Mr Morgan	153

1   England Expects

The rain fell to within ten feet of the ground and was then driven sideways by a near hurricane force 'lazy' wind that did not bother to go round, but went straight through the man standing beneath the large oak tree, in the middle of the ten acre field, in the pitch dark of a late November Welsh night.

The man tried to hide behind the tree, but the wind was on to that with the speed of a striking rattlesnake and simply veered round a point or two and sent its rain soaked lances once more through the light-weight, stylish raincoat, as though in derision at the flimsy, trendy but quite useless garment.

The man shuddered, feeling the rain running down inside his shirt collecting in a puddle round his once much admired Union Jack jockey shorts, then shooting out and down his trouser legs, for all the world as though he were a small boy left too long with his hand up after drinking several cans of lemonade.

He shuddered again and tried to think rationally of how he came to be here at all. It was by no means his normal scene, he liked bright lights, big cities with lots of clubs and pubs and fast cars, and people who spoke the good old understandable English language - yet here he was - and, if he was not very careful, very careful indeed, here he would stay - for somewhere out there in the dark, were two men with flat caps, funny accents, large wellies and two fully loaded shotguns - their one shared aim in life - to kill him.

His name was Rupert Courtney Morgan - he was thirty years old - tall, slimish - if you overlooked the embryo beer gut - blonde haired, blue eyed and terrified out of his mind. How had he got into this mess? Three weeks ago he was a happy man, holding down a safe yet romantic sounding job as a minor agent for the Department of Industrial Espionage (D.I.E.) - a very small offshoot of the big government departments who went in for the real thing, chasing Russian agents and mad would-be world dominators - jumping over the Berlin Wall with the ease and regularity of a London commuter - and whose agents were licensed to kill!

All Rupert was licensed to do was to drive cars of all sizes, motorised lawn mowers and anything included in Sections A, B and C, but not motor cycles. His job was to visit factories, workshops, small businesses and to advise on the dangers of industrial espionage - what it was and how to avoid it. It was surprising how few people realised that industrial espionage was a vast problem and on the increase - dress designs stolen before a collection can be shown - the plans of a new all gay action man for the toy market - even the design of a revolutionary condom stolen by a balloon manufacturer who had got hold of the wrong end of the stick.

Rupert liked his job - it was well paid and he could play at James Bond to his heart's content in perfect safety, hammering his three and a half litre supercharged battleship grey Bentley, cunningly disguised as a standard production line Mini Metro, round the romantic streets of West Putney - or parking it out by the kerb at night and collecting it from the pound the next day where it had been taken and strip-searched by the agents of SMERSH masquerading as London Coppers. It was a satisfying life, a happy life and there were prospects. By the time he was forty he would have his own office near Whitehall - but the other side of the river round by Vauxhall Bridge - noisy, but you felt you were in touch with the main arteries of the Nation.

Rupert had spent ten years with the Department, ten fun-filled peaceful years, telling the girls he was an agent for D.I.E. which usually impressed them enough to get them home - though not to meet Mother. She was safely tucked away in Basingstoke where she was the backbone of the W.I. and the back breaking bane of his father - who, according to his mother, had a 'practice' in Basingstoke. He was actually a peripatetic chiropodist - which meant he went round to people's houses and did things to their feet - but mother insisted it was a 'practice'. Rupert would most likely have never left home if he had been brought up in Eton, or Windsor - or even Rugby - but Basingstoke!

He never really knew why, but whenever he told anyone that he came from Basingstoke there was always the slight hint of a giggle or a snigger. So he lived in a two roomed flat on the third floor of a Victorian house on the outskirts of Putney. He paid a high rent but he did not mind - it was his own. It was decorated in a variety of styles - each reflecting the taste of a number of live-in girlfriends who seemed to leave before they could quite finish the job. Rupert had a secret theory that the girl who did complete the decor would be his wife - so often a little sabotage of his own would take place - he was not ready for the big blind date yet.

Yes, all was well with the world - he had spent his summer holidays in the South of France walking round the Casinos in a borrowed white dinner jacket, occasionally throwing the odd Franc carelessly onto the roulette table - and working hard at the sun tan that would enhance his stories about being abroad on an assignment.

The peace of his life had been shattered the day - was it really only three weeks ago? - when he was summoned to the Chief's office. It had been a normal day up to then, the casual drive into town, a short bloody death defying duel for a parking meter, the first cup of official department coffee that he always thought had been got at by a tea manufacturer with a grudge, a quick glance through the papers on his desk - the Sun, the Mirror and the Times - which was really only used to wrap around the other two when travelling - then a quiet contemplation of a lunch venue. Should he go into the city and mix with the newspaper men or up the Charing Cross Road and watch the gays bartering for afternoon brides! He had almost come down in favour of the City when the black telephone on his desk rang. He wished he could have one that bleeped or flashed a light or just purred - but his rang!

    He picked it up and his life changed - a cryptic message: get over to Whitehall at once, he was to see the Big Chief of D.I.E. straight away. Was this a mission? Should he check his passport and vaccinations? He strolled casually past the desks of the other agents and typists - quietly informed the Head of Section that he would be out for a while - and left the building wondering what the hell he had done that necessitated a personal interview with his Number One.

    He entered the impressive looking building on the unfashionable side of Whitehall and was immediately stopped by a uniformed commissionaire, with a look that had been perfected on the beaches of Dunkirk, when raw privates started crying for their mother. Rupert showed his Department Pass that so impressed the young females of West Putney.

    'Oh - that lot!' said the ex-Sergeant Major - in a tone that dismissed all civilians to the level of sheep. 'You got an 'happointment have you?' Rupert wanted to say 'Yes my man' but thought better of it and merely nodded - 'Wait here' - the sergeant indicated a spot on the polished tiled floor, Rupert stood on it, and knew he would not be able to move until told to do so.

Why, he wondered could he not be like some of the public school types in the department who would have simply ordered this red faced hero of the battle of the bulge to announce their arrival to the relevant office and would have elicited a crisp 'Yessir'. Rupert could never do that, all authority seemed to awe him slightly - he never knew why. In his own field he was confident enough, but men with uniforms and set ranks, and somehow a total belief in their rightness made him uneasy.

The sergeant, who had disappeared into one of those government office type tardises that always seem to be full of ex-soldiers, reappeared - stared hard at Rupert as though deciding whether or not he needed a haircut, and then - in crisp army-ese - said: 'Room Two oh fiver, fifther floorer, knock and wait - do not on any account get out of the lift at any other floor'. Rupert heard the unspoken order 'move' - thanked the sergeant and headed for the lifts.

The corridor leading to Room 205 was carpeted in a deep red deep pile carpet that had never been in a reduced sale in Wandsworth High Street. Rupert waded through it to the door; he knocked and as instructed, waited. It opened. Inside he could see a large desk resting on an even deeper pile carpet - a voice from the direction of the desk said 'Come in Morgan' - he did so and the door whispered shut behind him.

He stood, his ankles lost in the shaggy wool of the carpet, staring at the enormous desk - it was at least four times the size of any desk he had ever seen - he could not see over it or around it. From somewhere inside it came a voice: 'Sit down Morgan - I will be with you in a moment' He looked around - there were no chairs of any kind 'Sit on the floor' the voice said - 'not much point in having the most luxurious carpets in the country if you are just going to walk all over them. Oh and take your shoes off - will you - they do so much damage to the pile!'

Rupert sat. He removed his shoes as told and wondered what the hell was going on - was this really the head office of the department - was this how the really top people lived - and why hadn't he changed his socks this morning, instead of leaping into the pair he had been wearing for at least two days. Before he could answer any of these questions the Head of the department came out from under the desk and stared at Rupert.

Rupert stared back at the Chief - who was the most remarkable person he had ever seen - short - about five foot six - very thin, completely bald, pink, dressed only in a Gandhi type loin cloth and clutching a large shaggy black cat!

'So - you are Morgan' said the Chief.

'Yes sir' said Morgan, assuming the sex from the angle of the loin cloth.

'Good' sighed the Chief - as he lowered himself to the floor opposite Rupert - 'Good - how old are you?'

'Thirty' said Rupert

'Good' said the Chief, 'I am fifty-two and a half - a nice age you know.'

'Yes' said Rupert -

'Are you gay?' said the Chief

'No' said Rupert - not sure whether he was expected to be or not - it was a problem nowadays - it was so easy to upset people, or even lose your job if you either admitted to being gay or if you said that you were not, but as always when asked the question he tossed a mental coin - and hoped for the best. There was a pause - while the Chief looked hard at him.

'Are you sure' said he -

'Oh yes' said Rupert 'I mean I should know, I think, shouldn't I?' The Chief stroked the cat for a moment or two before answering, then, 'Not necessarily my boy, there are a lot of people around today who don't know whether they are coming or going, if you know what I mean.'

Rupert hesitated - 'Er - yes sir - I think I do...'

'I think therefore I am - eh? ', said the Chief

'What?' said Rupert, sufficiently stunned to forget his manners.

'Dustcarts' said the Chief - completely losing Rupert 'Anyway enough of the pleasantries - What do you know about Wales?'

'Er - pardon', he said - this time remembering his early school lessons -

'Wales?' said the Chief sharply, 'Wales?'

'Ah Whales' said Rupert - his mind racing. Whales? Yes, well they do say that they talk to each other sir - and that they sing as well - and well, we get a lot of blubber from them and - '

'Wales the country' sliced in the Chief 'not the fish - though if you have spent much time there you could be excused thinking -' he broke off - 'you have spent time there haven't you Morgan?'

'I have never been there in my life sir' said Rupert truthfully.

'What - never?' the Chief looked aghast 'but the computer - well I mean - you are Morgan - Junior Investigator D.I.E? R. C. Morgan?'

'Yes sir' said Rupert - puzzled.

'Vauxhall Bridge Section?' whispered the Chief - 'Yes sir' said Rupert - happy to know that the Chief had heard of him -

'And you say you have never spent any time in Wales?' said the Chief icily -

'None at all, sir, the nearest I ever got was watching the International at Twickenham, sir', gushed Rupert in the longest sentence he had uttered so far in the presence of his great boss - 'Wales lost sir!'

There was a long silence. Rupert stared at the carpet as the Chief stared at him.

'There seems to be some discrepancy here' said the Chief after enough time had elapsed to read War and Peace in Russian.

'Yes sir' said Rupert, hating not being able to conduct himself in true James Bond fashion.

'However' purred the Chief, 'Errors are not officially recognised in this Department - therefore - you will have to take the assignment.'

Assignment! That magic word - Assignment! Assignment Bangkok! Assignment Berlin! Assignment Leningrad! The sheer magic of the word rolled through Rupert's head. At last!

'Yes sir' he said - doing his best to raise himself up to his full proud height whilst sitting cross-legged and cramped in the carpet - 'My passport is in order - I have all the vaccinations - when do I leave and where do I fly to, sir?'

'You leave tomorrow, and you drive - destination Cardiff.'

Before Rupert could answer, the Chief raised the cat to his ear, pressed a hidden button somewhere in the region of the vets perks, and spoke - 'Bring in the file on Blanchard will you Miss Romanov' There was a muffled 'Yes sir' from the cat's mouth. The door opened - Miss Romanov entered. She was short and squat, she wore a severe grey suit, her hair was tied back in a bun, and small round National Health glasses perched on her hooked nose. She waded through the carpet and deposited a slim file at the feet of the Chief. He thanked her briefly and dismissed her. As she passed Rupert she winked, seductively - and left. Rupert ignored her - not knowing whether it was really a wink or a nervous twitch - in either case he did not intend to pursue the strange and totally un-alluring Miss Romanov. Romanov!!

'Yes - she is Russian' said the Chief - reading his thoughts, 'the best secretary I've ever had, and the only one I can truly trust - - if you think about it, it makes sense.' Rupert thought about it - it didn't!

'Well' said the Chief, 'the point is, I know that she is a spy, she knows I know, so she can't get any real information from my Department, but she likes London and especially the chain stores - so we have lunch together now and again - I tell her a few useless secrets and we are both happy; she doesn't have men problems either - perfect. Now...' - the Chief opened the file - Rupert slowly digested the last piece of information and it did make some sense, but he did suspect that Miss Romanov had some men problems, like having to shave twice a day for one. He shuddered; certain things did not bear thinking about. The Chief was talking again - 'Now Morgan' said the Chief - 'we have a serious problem in Wales.'

'Yes sir' said Rupert to show he was paying attention.

'A very serious problem' - the Chief hesitated, looked around the room to make sure they were alone - 'one of our senior agents has been found dead!'

Rupert stared at the Chief then stammered - 'Found dead sir?'

'Yes' said the Chief 'and if you are going to repeat everything I say - make sure it is only in this room, you understand?'

'Oh yes sir. Was this, er agent - murdered or something, sir?' Rupert was beginning to feel a little bit nervous now, after all he was not a trained field agent in M.I.5 - or anything like that - was he - and death - well that was sort of permanent. The Chief looked at him sharply - then said very quietly 'What made you say that Morgan, do you know something I should know?'

'No - of course not' said Rupert, wondering why he had said 'murdered' too.

'Good' whispered the Chief, 'as long as we know where we stand - now listen!' He edged closer to Rupert until he was almost touching his knee - Rupert's mind raced - was this the moment of truth? What should he do if it was? The Chief's hand was on his knee now, oh - to hell with it - he thought - there is too much unemployment around - I am not going to join the dole queue - better bed than dead - lie back and think of Basingstoke!

'Morgan!' snapped the Chief -'are you quite well - I need your entire attention!'

'Oh yes sir' Rupert almost squealed 'sorry sir, it was the thought of death sir!'

'Quite' said the Chief eyeing Morgan curiously. Rupert nodded - half closing his eyes to indicate total attention.

'Our Man Blanchard' said the Chief - in a low conspiratorial tone - 'was found two days ago in his car high on the side of a Welsh mountain - a plastic tube was running from the exhaust pipe to the driver's window, the engine had stopped, Blanchard was dead!'

Rupert looked serious - Ah - he thought - then - Ah again! 'So - it was suicide then sir?' he said - with all the confidence of a Dr. Watson.

'Ah!' said the Chief - 'that's what we thought at first, but there are some details that puzzle us - that is why we want you to go down to Wales and find out all you can about poor Blanchard's last hours!'

'Oh I see!' said Rupert 'May I ask, sir, what are the strange details you mentioned?'

The Chief looked at Rupert for a moment then: 'Are you sure you are not gay?'

'Yes' said Rupert - his voice rising to a girlish falsetto at the suddenness of the question - 'Why?' he spluttered - an octave lower -

'Blanchard was' said the Chief 'and we don't want what ever happened to him to happen to you - do we?'

'You think his death had something to do with his - er - his er...?' said Rupert, not quite sure how to phrase what he meant - which was sex-life.

'More a case of his *im*' said the Chief, and there was a hint of a smile on his face. Rupert stared - the man was human - or was he just testing. 'In any event' the Chief went on - 'there was definitely something queer about his death!'

Was it his imagination or was the Chief really being flippant, or thought Rupert, was fifty-two and a half old enough to use the word 'queer' in the old-world sense? Life seemed to Rupert to be full of problems this morning

'Quite so - sir' he said - opting for good, safe ground 'what exactly was there that makes it seem that way, sir?' he said, playing even safer -

'The fact' said the Chief 'that between the poor man's legs were a copy of Under Milk Wood by Dylan Thomas, and a large leek!'

'Oh!' said Rupert. There wasn't much else he could say.

'And' - went on the Chief 'he was clutching in his arms a deflated rugby ball'

'Oh' said Rupert again - for the same reason he'd said it last time.

'And', continued the Chief, 'scrawled across the windscreen of his car was the one word - Megan!'

'Ah!' said Rupert - fearing that his conversation was getting boring -

'What do you make of that then?' asked the Chief - staring intently at Rupert. Rupert thought hard - then -

'I don't know sir - as you say - very queer!'

'Yes indeed!' The Chief stood up looking down on Rupert. Rupert realised that the interview was nearly over, and reached for his shoes -

'Get down there' said the Chief briskly - 'find out all you can and report back to me directly - all right? Any questions?'

'Only one, sir' asked Rupert tentatively 'Why me sir?'

The Chief gave Rupert a long glance, then - 'Because you are the only man in the Department with a Welsh sounding name - of course!' At this - he turned and disappeared into his desk.

2   Across Offa's Dyke.

For a few seconds the rain eased, Rupert tried to look out from behind the tree to see if he could catch sight of his pursuers - but there was not a thing to be seen nor a sound to be heard over the howling wind, and such complete darkness was something that Rupert had never experienced before, having been brought up in the constant glow of street lights. He shivered remembering how excited he'd been on that first day of his mission.

The Chief had left instructions with Miss Romanov for Rupert, he was to stay at the Harp Hotel in Cardiff and all his reasonable expenses would be paid. As soon as he arrived there he was to make himself known to the local office - the address of which he was handed along with a copy of the details of poor Blanchard's demise. As he left, Miss Romanov winked at him again - and again he was not sure about the reason for her doing so, so he nodded as though he understood what it was she was trying to communicate to him and went down in the lift, remembering not to get out at any other floor until the ground floor - where he passed the monument to British Sergeant-hood almost jauntily - and so out into the street.

He was on a mission - Assignment Cardiff. Alright it was only to Wales but up to now the furthest he had travelled for the Department was Walthamstow to give a talk to the local young wives' club, though why they wanted to know about industrial espionage had been beyond him. From the way they had behaved that afternoon a short sharp lecture on the purpose, practise and history of the chastity belt would have made more sense. But now he was on his first real assignment, it had everything - death - intrigue... he must go and buy a copy of Under Milk Wood - he thought... sex, if indeed Megan was a woman and not some sort of code word - yes this was real life. Pity about the Mini Metro but then nothing was perfect and it was better than being got there on a Virgin Train. He had packed his trendiest gear, he wanted to impress the country folk of Wales with his London sophistication - and having told a friendly neighbour that he would be away for a day or so - he set off in his car for Wales – 'Land of our Fathers'.

The journey was uneventful - apart from an embarrassing moment or two with a do-it-yourself petrol pump just outside Monmouth - Rupert was the first to admit that he was not good with anything mechanical - the proprietors had been very good about it and said that they could soon wash away the excess petrol that he had spilt because of reading the wrong section of the pump - but he would have to pay for the amount the pump had discharged - which he did, hoping that there would be enough time during the mission to explain away twenty gallons of petrol for one trip in a mini metro.

He reached Monmouth and crossed Offa's Dyke into Wales in excellent time - it was only as he was entering Merthyr Tydfil that he realised that something was wrong - he had not seen a sign indicating Cardiff for some time, and he couldn't read most of the road signs anyway for the English section had been painted over with green paint leaving only a jumble of meaningless words. It was Rupert's first example of the country's little foibles - a land where the majority language was English, yet because of a very small minority of avid Welsh speakers all road signs and most official forms had to be printed in both languages, thus causing much extra cost to a nation claiming it was in great need of money, and a great deal of confusion to non-Welsh speaking Welshmen and foreigners alike.

It certainly confused Rupert who had in the end to park his car and go in search of a policeman to help him as his road map was not bilingual. After spending ten minutes trying to make himself understood to a passing stranger - who was, as it happened, a non-English speaking Dane on holiday in Wales - Rupert finally found a police station and was put on the right track by the policeman who walked back with him to his car and booked him for not displaying his road tax - the fact that Rupert explained to him that in London he always locked his tax disc in the glove compartment because round Putney area it would probably get nicked - made no impact on the local policeman - who promptly switched to Welsh when warning Rupert, so that he never knew whether he had been properly booked or not.

Rupert reached Cardiff at six in the evening, after the rush hour. It was very quiet, so quiet that it worried him. However he found the Harp - a quaint Victorian hotel, with quaint Victorian rooms but very new Elizabethan prices. He checked out his room for bugs and for any listening devices, then trekked down the corridor to the bathroom, then trekked back as it was occupied - when he re-entered his room he checked the hairs that he had stretched across the catch of his suitcase. They had not been moved - he was vaguely disappointed. He noticed the small portable colour T.V. that stood in the corner of the room - he switched on - almost instantly the room was filled with a fierce guttural sounding babble, as the picture came up he saw that it was a rugby match being described in Welsh by a very enthusiastic commentator. Quickly Rupert pressed a button on the side of the T.V. - here was the same match but being described in the dulcet tones of a B.B.C. English sports commentator. Rupert watched for a while thinking that this may not be Leningrad but with the different language and all, it was certainly a foreign country, and that pleased him.

He contemplated dinner - he decided - in true agent fashion that he would go for the local dishes. He believed that one should try these things - in France he had spent two days in bed after a plate of grilled squid and frog's legs in white wine, but he was quite sure that it had been the water in his room that had caused his colon to try tying reef knots.

He wondered on reflection whether he should drink the water here in Wales. His parents wouldn't touch water from a tap anywhere outside a three mile radius of Basingstoke - then he remembered that he had read about Welsh water being supplied to many parts of England so he assumed that it would be all right. After finally gaining access to the bathroom and splashing the latest wonder woman-baiter lotion all over himself, he dressed in a pair of light grey casual slacks, a blue shirt with matching tie, a light pig skin leather coat - made in Israel - which still bore a well-known chain store label hanging out the back of the collar. He slipped his feet into a pair of black shoes - leather uppers man-made soles - he pocketed a fresh pack of the world's best-selling cigarettes, checked that his Zippo was loaded - did a couple of quick practise trick strikes and he was ready for whatever pleasures Cardiff could offer him on that grey October night.

He was surprised to discover that the saloon bar of the hotel was open to non-residential customers, and soon found himself in the midst of a motley crowd of office workers, road menders, drunks, doctors and insurance salesmen - the last of which were attending a conference in the hotel and whose conversation was punctuated with such words as 'prospects' 'mortality rates' 'endowments' and 'gin and tonic Nigel please'. One of them, thought

Rupert was one of the group, which annoyed him somewhat - but when the errant salesman found that Rupert was not a fellow conferencee, he tried to sell him life assurance - which annoyed Rupert even more.

Finding an empty stool at the end of the bar Rupert sat and studied the scene. Nowhere in London, he thought, could you see such a mixture of types in one bar. In towns, people of a like nature and occupation tended to form together and use their own pubs - obviously this did not apply here in the land of male voice choirs and rugby. This last thought had entered his mind because, while he had been contemplating the customers, a small section had started to sing. Ah! - thought Rupert - the local night life was starting. He was wrong, however, for the group had only managed to get through half a verse of 'Bread of Heaven' sung at full strength, off key and flat, when two burly looking chaps moved in and ushered them out.

There was a small affray - then all was quiet again. Rupert sipped his cold lager, and wondered at the way that no-one in the bar had taken any notice of the event but had just gone on drinking and talking their own forms of shop. It is a fact of life in the twentieth century that in civilised society one has to do something totally outrageous to even lift the eyebrows of one's fellow man. Nobody wants to look foolish, so they ignore everything - just in case it might be the new in-thing. Rupert was no different, worse in a way - for he was in a foreign land and did not know the local customs. After two more lagers he decided to make his way to the dining room - it was here he had his first brush with a bi-cultural state.

The restaurant itself was pleasing enough - if a little old fashioned for Rupert's taste. He showed his room key and number and was shown to a table that seemed to be perfect for anyone wishing not to be noticed, tucked away behind a plastic palm tree and within close proximity to the wash room door - which was very handy, thought Rupert, as the first of the lager started working its way through his system. The loud musak from the speaker directly above his head actually pleased him, as it would be difficult for anyone to overhear any conversation of a secret nature that might take place at his table in the coming days - all in all, it was a good set-up, thought Rupert.

The waitress pushed a menu at him and disappeared again. He studied it with much interest looking for any indigenous dishes, but he could see none - unless leeks-au-gratin were solely a Welsh vegetable - which he doubted. He decided to ask the waitress, if and when she returned. During the long wait he contemplated the task ahead of him. He had decided that as he was so late in getting to Cardiff he would contact the local office in the morning, when he was fresh. He took from his pocket a small card on which was written the name and address of the local man - 'Iestyn Morris'. He did not know how to pronounce that first name but someone should be able to tell him before he went to the meeting. The waitress returned - 'You want to order now?' she sighed, with an air that said - 'I've been waiting long enough, you know!'

'Oh, yes' said Rupert - mustering what sophistication he could - 'What would you recommend that is of a genuine Welsh character?' The waitress stared at him as though he were quite mad - 'The chef is French' she said 'most of the food is French - we don't do Welsh food, not that there is much of it anyway - except cawl and laver bread!'

'Ah!' said Rupert - 'then I will have the soup of the day and you can bring ne a couple of slices of laver bread to go with it.'

'It don't come in slices!' said the waitress, 'it - '

'Never mind how it comes' said Rupert suavely, 'just bring me some with the soup' - and before the waitress could say anything he went on to order a sirloin steak and chips, as he did not have very good memories of French cooking.

The waitress left, muttering to herself something about 'loony Englishmen' and a wine waiter in a stained jacket came up to his table and thrust a wine list at Rupert, who ordered a pint of chilled lager and half a bottle of red wine. The wine waiter slouched off leaving Rupert feeling somewhat dissatisfied with the service but unable to say exactly why - most foreign countries were glad of the influx of sterling into their economy - but here he was - an Englishman abroad - and being treated - he thought - with complete lack of enthusiasm - if not hostility. This latter thought was confirmed when his soup arrived accompanied by a plate of the most disgusting looking black goo he had ever seen.

'What is this?' he almost yelled -

'Soup and laver bread like you ordered, sir' said the waitress without looking at him - 'though how you can eat that horrible stuff with or without soup, is beyond me!'

She started to leave - 'But, what is it made of?' said Rupert, whose colon was having total recall of boiled squid and frogs legs -

'Seaweed of course' said the waitress over her shoulder as she simpered past the wine waiter, who sniggered his way to Rupert's table - glanced at the laver bread, almost openly laughed and went off in pursuit of the waitress.

Again, Rupert felt that the service left a great deal to be desired. It struck him that if this was the Welsh at their most sophisticated - what would it be like when he had to travel to the interior - as he most surely would have to do - to find the secret of poor Blanchard's death.

'You gay then, are you?' The question came from a large cupboard in the corner of an office, that looked and smelled as if it doubled at night as a boarding kennel for un-house-trained dogs.

'No, I am not!' yelled Rupert at the door of the cupboard - making a mental note to change his hairstyle and have a good look at his wardrobe when he got back to London. At the moment he felt tired, very tired. The night at the Harp Hotel had not been restful, as twenty or thirty drunken life assurance men had been rampaging up and down the corridors until breakfast time - one of them had spent an hour outside Rupert's room pleading to be let in and forgiven by someone called Robert. When Rupert emerged for breakfast - lying across the doorway was a sleeping figure wearing only a pair of bright green Y-fronts - Rupert stepped over the body carefully not to wake it.

Breakfast was much like dinner the night before, but without the musak and the wine waiter. Rupert had opted for the traditional English breakfast, as it was his opinion you couldn't go far wrong with that. He was surprised, however, at the total error of his belief. He left the hotel with two objectives in mind - one to visit the local office of D.I.E. and two, to find another hotel.

He had found the local office easily enough, stuck as it was at the end of a dark alley, way down by the docks of Cardiff... two flights of stairs had to be climbed before arriving at the door, which was marked: 'Simon Cranes - Manager - Knock and Enter'. He did so, and there was no-one in the office - then the voice from the cupboard - and the offensive question…

A short dark man, almost as broad as he was tall, emerged from inside the cupboard. He wore a dark blue suit, black shoes, white shirt - a club tie of some sort. His dark hair fell in a lump over his right eye, as he spoke he shifted it back into place, checking a sort of hair clip at the same time. He gave Rupert a look that almost dared him to notice the toupee - and walked around to his desk - which was of a normal size - as a consequence when he sat behind it, he all but vanished from sight. 'Iestyn Morris' he said, pronouncing his first name - 'Yes tin' - 'You're Morgan?' He stood up and extended his hand - Rupert took it - then handed it back complete with its leather glove, as Iestyn sat down and burst into laughter.

'Just my little joke, Morgan - breaks the ice eh?'

'Yes, of course' said Rupert - as he watched the Welshman screw the false hand back into its socket.

'Hope you don't mind the smell of dogs, Morgan bach' he said 'I keep the greyhounds here some nights when I've been racing them, see?'

'Yes, of course.' said Rupert, mentally naming the Welshman the Leggo-man.

'Like the cover firm on the door there, Morgan bach? Real firm, you know!'

'Of course' said Rupert, determined that next time he would not say - of course!

'Have any trouble finding the place then?' said Morris, diving under the desk and picking up what looked like a pair of pink briefs -

'No!' said Rupert, with relief 'Actually everyone seemed to know where you were!'

'Iestyn the spy, eh? That's what they call me - bloody silly!' snorted Morris -

'Yes, that's what they said!' uttered Rupert.

Morris looked at him sharply, then smiled - 'Aye, aye' he said - then for no apparent reason said 'Yes, yes!'

'You know why I am here - don't you Mr Morris?' asked Rupert

'Call me Iestyn' said Morris - 'Yes, I know why you are here, bach' - he adjusted his wig again - sat back in the chair and said, after a pause - 'Nasty business!' - he paused again - 'Nasty business, bach!'

Rupert was very puzzled. Although there had been a time, during his twenties, when a number of people had thought he looked like a young Michael Caine - no-one had ever before likened him to the great German composer - yet here was this round Welshman openly calling his Bach by the minute.

'Nasty business, yes' went on Morris 'yes! Nice bloke Blanchard' said Morris 'if you overlooked his little problem...'

'I'm afraid I never knew him' said Rupert 'and I know nothing about him - perhaps you could tell me exactly what he was working on, and what happened?'

'As to what happened' said Morris 'I don't know any more than you do - but as to what he was working on - well, there's another mystery - I mean he wasn't on a mission' - he used the word derisively - 'he was only going around giving the standard lectures on the job, you know' - Rupert looked sharply at Morris, but there did not seem to be any double meaning in what he had said -

'I see' - he said 'But wasn't there anything at all off-beat about the last few days - I mean, did he seem depressed or anything?'

Morris thought for a minute, then - 'Well, you know with old Blanchard it was hard to tell, he was nearly always depressed...but no' he went on 'he wasn't any more depressed than usual...' He paused for a moment - 'I shall miss him, you know - this trouble will mean I shall have to go out and do the lectures myself - damned inconvenient - I mean I've got myself organised here -' he looked at Rupert suddenly - 'Unless they are going to post you here, is it?'

'Oh no' said Rupert hastily 'No, no, I was only sent down to find out what happened and to clear things up - you know - relatives - insurance - that sort of thing.'

'He didn't have any!' said Morris sulkily -

'Which?' said Rupert -

'Either!' muttered Morris -

'Oh!' said Rupert - 'Well, that only leaves finding out about what happened up in the mountains, doesn't it?'

'Yes' said Morris 'The police are the ones you want - Sergeant Evans will put you in touch with the local boys who found Blanchard.'

Morris rose and went to his cupboard - there was a slight clink of glass and he emerged - 'Well, what else do you want then - you London bastard?' shouted Morris - at a totally confused Rupert - 'Got what you came for, didn't you?' Rupert realised that Morris was drunk

'No-one ever cares about what happens down here, Butty, no-one!' shouted Morris 'No-one, not until one of you bloody English gets killed - then down you come blaming poor Iestyn - oh sod it!' Morris leapt up - went into the cupboard and came back out clutching a bottle of whisky -

'You might as well know, bach, I drink! I suppose you will report that to your fancy bosses in London, eh?' He sank into his chair lifting the bottle to his lips - Rupert was not sure what he should do - but thought it might be a good idea to find out about this Bach business.

'Mr Morris?' he said and then remembered - 'Er - Iestyn - why do you keep calling me Bach? My name is

Rupert Morgan, and I don't play any musical instruments?' There was a long pause, while Iestyn digested this statement, then he stared at Rupert, and smiled -

'It's a term of endearment, Rupert bach!' - he laughed - 'A term of endearment - only we use it all the time, even if we don't like the sods we are talking to, see?' He took another great gulp from the bottle, then - 'Bach? It means - small - little one - Rupert my little one? Term of endearment, that's all.'

Morris started to cry softly, whilst trying to sing 'Bread of Heaven' - he slumped forward onto the desk, getting more and more indistinct. Rupert walked to the door - he turned - knowing that good manners bade him thank Iestyn - but by now the Welshman was beginning to snore - so Rupert just waved his hand and tiptoed out of the room.

Sergeant Evans was a different kind of Welshman altogether from poor Iestyn. Big - very big - broad - extremely broad - he spoke with the clipped accents of a sergeant-major - which, indeed, he had been at one time - in the military police, of course. He stood six feet two inches tall and weighed sixteen stone - none of it fat - well, not more than two stone of it. He looked across at Rupert who was standing in the doorway of Cardiff's main police station - that smelled of stale beer and after-shave, mixed with a sprinkle of fish and chips.

'One of the dead man's boyfriends, are you?' boomed the sergeant - glaring at Rupert with that look of loathing all overt heterosexual men have when faced with the middlesex and are not too sure of their own deepest feelings -

'No, I am not!' Rupert said, with as much indignity as he could muster - 'I am from the Department of

Industrial Espionage, Head Office, London!' He handed one of his cards across to the sergeant who took it carefully by a small corner, and placed it in front of him on the counter, which stood between him and Rupert -

'Oh yes,' said the big man - 'the spy who came into the cold, eh?'

'From' said Rupert, who had read the book -

'What did you say?' said the sergeant with menace -

'Out of the cold' said Rupert 'The spy who came in from the cold!' The sergeant glared at him as though wondering just what faked charge he could book him on -

'Oh, I do beg your pardon!' - he falsely simpered - 'please forgive the ignorance of a poor humble country bobby - won't you Mr Bond - it is James Bond isn't it? Oh, Oh, seven, is it? Licensed to offend policemen in the pursuit of their duty - is it?' He came out from behind the counter - Rupert was appalled at the size of the man, and he was meant to be on the side of the angels!

'Now you listen to me - little man' the sergeant towered over Rupert and breathed second-hand mild and bitter directly into his face - 'Your little pansy friend topped himself up on the Beacons after a row with one of his fairy friends in the city. Why, I do not know - how can one ever know about you types eh? But that is what happened - suicide while the balance of his mind was disturbed - see??'

Rupert stared at the sergeant, wondering why the man was so vehement - what had he to hide - and why was he so vindictive against gays - - and how could he change his own image??

'There was no sign of foul play' continued the sergeant - 'unless you call slashing a rugby ball a foul - which many might do I suppose - but otherwise a straight case - pardon the joke - of suicide - - got it?'

'But then, who was - or is - Megan?' stammered Rupert determined not to be completely browbeaten -

'Probably some sort of code name for his lover' said the policeman, who had obviously lost interest in the matter -

'But you can't just lose interest in the matter like this' said Rupert - annoyed -

'Oh, now you are telling me what I can and cannot do eh?' grimaced the policeman - reaching for a copy of Burkes Law to see if this was an arrestable offence -

'No, I am not!' said Rupert - 'What I meant was - is - that there must be some more information you can give me to go on...'

The sergeant put down the book as his eyes could not quite focus on the small print - 'Look he said, and Rupert was taken aback at the almost friendly tone of the word - 'Look' repeated the policeman 'I'll tell you what I will do. If you are determined to make a fool of yourself, I will give you a letter of introduction to the officer in charge of the area where the dead man was found - you can go up there and see for yourself, where it happened - not that that will tell you anything of course - but it will keep you happy - won't it? And it will get you out of my hair - - O.K. bach?'

Rupert was amazed, it was quite the longest speech that had been made to him since he had been in Wales - 'Thank you' - he stammered - 'thank you very much - I should like that - if it would not be too much trouble.' He thanked the sergeant -

'No trouble at all, bachen' said the sergeant, adding another word to Rupert's Welsh collection - 'Just take a seat while I have my constable type you out a letter'.

Rupert sat. He did not see the look on the sergeant's face as he turned toward an inner office - which was a good thing - for apart from looking thoroughly evil, the sergeant had a nasty spot on the left side of his nose - and Rupert had a horror of acne…

It was lunch time when Rupert emerged from the police station clutching a small manila envelope addressed to a police inspector - D T Thomas in the town of Brecon, in the county of Powys - which he was informed was only forty odd miles from Cardiff. He returned to his hotel, collected his belongings and booked out - thankful that he would not have to spend another night avoiding life assurance…

Having been told that he was heading for the wild country, he invested in a pair of new string gloves and a bottle of scotch - to help avoid any trouble with the local water supply… The gloves would help him control the car better as he battled with the dangerous hair-pin bends he had been warned about, and anyway, they made him feel more like a rally driver and/or a secret agent. He felt happy as he set forth up the valleys to his unknown destination - his appointment with fate.

He would not have felt quite so happy if he could have read a certain fax that was at that moment wending its way to a certain solicitor's office in the town of Brecon in the county of Powys - the contents would have been enough to make him think more than twice about his journey - but the signature would have terrified him - for the fax was signed - 'Megan'…

3   Far Flung out-posts of the Empire

The rain had stopped and the wind had ceased its imitation of a sand blaster - Rupert sank to his knees hugging the side of the tree - he listened hard but could hear no sound of his pursuers. He leaned back on the trunk and looked up at the sky - a few stars were showing. He hoped that the moon would not come out - his light raincoat would be seen for miles - he wondered how long the men would keep searching. Soberly he thought, that with the knowledge he now had, they could not afford to let him escape - that bloody knowledge - he knew now - and wished he didn't - they could not let him reach 'Megan'.

It had been a bright starry night when he had first entered Brecon, although he had left Cardiff in good time for the forty mile journey. He had spotted a road sign that pointed to a rather narrow looking road and was clearly printed Brecon. The scenic route thought Rupert and imagining that he was driving through the wild wastes of central Russia - got thoroughly lost and stuck on a cattle grid high up on the Beacons. After much pushing and heaving and a little help from a group of S.A.S. trainees he was able to release his front wheel from the grid and speed off through the dusk towards Brecon, not knowing that he was now on the S.A.S. file of grade three suspected strangers and that his photo was at that moment being relayed to S.A.S. Headquarters for verification. He was happy in his ignorance and looking forward to a good meal and a drink...

The Old Boot Hotel in Brecon was the remains of a once grand hostelry - known for its service, cuisine and ostlers who were unsurpassed in their handling of even the most difficult horses, but alas no more. The only resemblance between the old days and now was that the steak Rupert ordered in the faded glory of the dining room tasted of and had the consistency of horse; the bedroom was Victorian and the plumbing original. Why was it - Rupert thought - that in Bond's world the lobster was always just chilled enough, the vodka perfect, and the waitresses willing and beautiful. Was it just his imagination or was the waitress at his table really the twin of the one in Cardiff?? Even to the same small black-head on the tip of her nose. Rupert finished his meal and the bottle of house wine that could have doubled for the vinegar and made his way to the lounge bar, hoping to kill the memory of the food with good, cold, foreign lager.

The bar was empty as Rupert entered; three lonely looking bar stools stood huddled together at one end of the counter, wooden memorials to a lunch time session. Rupert perched on one of them and waited for someone to come and take his order. He waited, and he waited! No-one came. Then he spied a small hand bell tucked away behind a soda siphon - he picked it up and waved it, it let out a plaintive 'ding-ding' - he put it down and again he waited...

Within a minute a smart looking dark haired young man in a purple jacket - with a motif of a boot on the pocket - appeared from somewhere in the dark recesses of the bar - he stared at Rupert as though at a man from outer space -

'Hello - how did you get there then?' he spoke in a deep dark Welsh accent -

'I am a resident' said Rupert' I have just come from the dining room' -

'Ah' sighed the barman 'have a meal did you?'

'Well - yes' said Rupert -

'Then I bet you need a drink - right?'

'You win' said Rupert - who was not by nature a gambling man 'could I have a pint of lager please?'

'One pint of cold lager coming up, sir' the barman repeated into the inner depths of the bar, leaving Rupert alone and wondering what it was about cheerful barmen that really got up his nose! He peered around the lounge, at the soft imitation velvet seating, the copper topped tables, the prints of race horses on the flock wallpaper - red of course, he had seen blue once and a very nasty green but on the whole flock wall paper was red.

'One pint of lager, sir' jollied the barman, making Rupert jump -

'90p sir - shocking price innit?'

Not when you are used to paying over a pound in London thought Rupert, but agreed with the barman - 'Yes! Everything is very expensive nowadays!' Bond of course, would have dismissed the barman by now, but Rupert did not know how to -

'You on holiday are you?' asked the barman - running a dirty cloth over the clean bar top.

'No' replied Rupert and then thought again - it would not do for him to tell the world what he was doing here. 'That is - yes - sort of' he corrected 'I am having a look round for a possible property - for a friend in London' - he hoped the barman would be impressed when he mentioned London.

'London eh?' sighed the barman wistfully 'I was up there, Soho you know - working in a pub - The Blue Posts – do you know it?'

Rupert was once more thrown into despair, he did not know the pub but he did not want this common barman to think he didn't know his London - why did it always happen to him - thought Rupert - why couldn't this minion be straight off the farm and all agog at this man about town from the capital city - no - Rupert had to meet a barman who not only knew London but had worked in Soho - an area Rupert tended to avoid as his Chinese was still limited to numbers.

'The Blue Posts' he said reflectively - 'yes I think I know it - not really my stamping ground you know!'

'Great pub it was -' enthused the barman 'a great pub, used to get all the tarts and gangsters in there when they was off duty like, real nice people too - when you got to know them'. This last was said with an air of deep knowledge. 'Not your scene though eh? You more the Kings Road touch eh? Well I used to pop down to the worlds end now and then but I didn't like it much, too many...'

He stopped suddenly - looked at Rupert 'Oh - look I'm sorry if I...well - you know - live and let live isn't it? - ' he paused, 'yea - great place London - I loved it...' He started to attack polished glasses with the cloth - now giving them a smear each.

Inwardly Rupert had just pulled the barman over the counter - delivered a short lecture on manners - punctuated with a sharp rap on the nose - outwardly he said -'Yes I know what you mean - but I spend most of my time in Putney!'

Rupert knew it was a totally crass statement but at that moment all he wanted was to be rid of this troublesome barman - who was just about to embark on what Rupert was sure was going to be an in-depth description of fifteen pubs in Putney - when into the bar walked a tall grey-haired gentleman - there was no other way to describe him - smartly dressed in cavalry twill trousers, sports jacket, soft check shirt, woollen tie - perched below a square military face which sported the very thinnest and whitest hint of a moustache. He strode purposefully towards Rupert - but was intercepted by the barman. 'Ah - good evening Brigadier' - he said cheerfully -'The usual is it?'

'Evening Ianto', barked the Brig - 'If you please' - then turned and eyed Rupert as though working out if he was officers' mess material -

'Good evening young man' he said, friendly enough.

'Good evening sir' said Rupert, without knowing why he called the man - sir - there was just something about the fellow that made him call him sir - he hated himself for doing so - but did it never the less.

'Forgive an old man's indulgences - will you young man' smiled the Brigadier 'but I always sit in that corner on that stool - you know?'

Rupert was amazed - and as always when he was amazed he stammered - 'I - er - that is - I mean - sorry!'

'It's quite true, sir - always sits there he does' piped in the barman as he placed a large gin and tonic beside Rupert's pint - 'Silly to be such a creature of habit - I know - but there it is' the Brigadier gave Rupert a look that said 'I have served me country through two world wars, you know, not much to ask a bit of privilege in me old age - what?'

It was the longest sentence Rupert had ever seen - or heard - in a look. He got off the stool - took another and moved - with his pint - to the other end of the small bar.

'Many thanks' gushed the Brigadier 'Many thanks indeed – I can see you are a gentleman - been in the services have you?'

'No sir' answered Rupert, thinking it wise not to mention his adventures in the combined cadet force at school -

'Royal Engineers, you know' stated the Brig, not really hearing Rupert's answer 'served through two world wars, couple of bangs - but nothing serious you know - flesh wounds - that's all!'

Rupert stared at him aghast, for he knew what was about to happen and he could not think of any way of avoiding it - he almost longed for the barman and his inane talk of London low life and pubs.... he nodded an 'oh really' to the Brig, hoping against hope that there might be some reprieve - but no - a quick professional swig at the gin and tonic - a glance to confirm that he had a virgin audience and the Brig was off, as indeed was the barman - into his dark retreat.

'Wouldn't think it to look at me - would you - but I'm seventy-nine next month' -

'Never' - Rupert smiled - he knew it was expected of him... The Brig's voice droned on, as Rupert half listening, considered the thought that had just come into his head - it was his opinion that one could probably walk into almost any country pub in England, Scotland or Wales - and probably Northern Ireland too - and ask for the Brigadier, the Captain or the Major - and be told either than he would be in 'later' or had 'just left'.

'India you know...' the Brig's voice swam to the surface of Rupert's mind - it would have to be bloody India he thought. 'When the Khyber Pass meant more than a crude piece of rhyming slang - what?' the Brig laughed at his little joke - and plunged on...

Yes, that would be it - thought Rupert - the reason for them all being out in the sticks... To the old soldiers the hills of Wales or Scotland would be a bit like the hills above Ranjipur or whatever - and with their failing sight and hearing, the dark heads of the Celts and the foreign sounding language could make them feel that they were back in the good old days of the Raj - polo ponies - tiffin - bungalows and Gunga-bloody-din....

'Course you couldn't find a finer fighting man in all the world' rasped the hero of the trenches 'despite their colour - damned loyal too' -

Rupert sank back into his storm room of thought - wondering if all over India there were Indian Captains and Majors boring the chapattis off the young lads in the beetle-nut bars... with 'Never mind their sweaty pink faces and the strange smell of them, Mr. Patel, I am telling you they were damned fine soldiers - in they would go - with their tally-hoes and 'up and at em lads' - swords flying - guns banging - and in we would go too - right behind them - picking up the bits - oh yes - they were brave men!'

'Well we knew the Bosch were just over the next ridge - don't you know...' Rupert started - which war was the old warrior on now... he nodded knowingly -'I'm not boring you - I hope' said the Brig with no hint of noticing Rupert's lack of attention - 'I do tend to be a bit of a bore you know…'

Why oh why - screamed Rupert in his head - couldn't he shout...Yes you are boring the arse off me - you anachronistic old fool - I don't care about the bloody war - there are more important things going on now, and you stopped thinking somewhere around the beaches of Normandy - I am very grateful - really I am - we all are - all us young people - for what you bloodthirsty old soldiers have done for us - but we are young and we must live for the future... I am sorry!...

'Not at all, sir' he said 'please don't think that - I am fascinated - really!' Rupert squirmed as he heard the words coming out of his mouth.

'Ah well' beamed the Brig 'That's splendid - let's have another noggin and I'll tell you how we got out of that bit of bother'... On, on, and on it droned - more beer stops - then on again - until unbelievingly - the Brig was getting up - doing up his coat - making going-away noises - 'Well young man' he said cheerily, 'like your company, but can't keep your hours - the old bones need the rest - don't you know?' Rupert smiled wanly. 'I must say I have really enjoyed our little chat - if you are around for a few days I will tell you some more...' He shook Rupert by the hand and went out of his life as smoothly as he had come into it.

Rupert sat numb! His hand clutching a full pint - he looked around the bar, surprised to see that it was now quite full. He looked at his watch, it was still early evening, he couldn't have spent more than an hour with the bloodthirsty Brigadier who, as he had told Rupert was directly related via deed poll to the Great Duke of Wellington. Rupert wondered if the two world wars had seemed so long to the combatants - probably not - he thought, for they at least could fire back... at the enemy. He was contemplating the state of the human race when a loud beery Welsh voice exploded in his left ear -

'I see you met old shotgun Wesley' - Rupert turned to face a cheery looking red faced, overweight, dark haired man -

'I'm sorry?' muttered Rupert - not sure whether the man was talking to him or not - 'Shotgun Wesley!' emphasised the man - 'You know - the old buggerdere!' - he paused - 'We call him shotgun 'cos he's a right twelve bore, see?'

'Ah yes' sighed Rupert - somehow a sixth sense deep in the bowels of his subconscious was telling him an old cliché about frying pans and fires -

'Not a bad old boy really mind, fair play' said the Welshman 'He did fight in the wars too' - he laughed loud and shouted 'Mind you we're not sure whose side he was on!' He roared with laughter at this obviously well tried joke. Rupert smiled politely. 'Don't mind me' choked the Welshman as he came down off his peak of hysteria, 'Just my sense of humour, see? - You English are you?' He fired from the hip.

'Er - yes - I am' stammered Rupert... here nearly added - 'and I'm not gay' but thought that he was too young to start getting paranoid.

'Thought so' said the Welshman - pleased with himself 'I can always spot an Englishman - down on holiday are you? Bit late in the year in'it? You should have been here in the summer man - beautiful it is then... Cold now though - you like fishing?'

Rupert thought painfully that he was destined to be the one always picked out by drunks and loonies - and people with a life story to tell. What - he wondered - was it he had that made him such perfect target for these twilight people - was it a fellow feeling? No - he never told anyone his life story - if he started he would be soon over-ridden and told to shut up and not be silly - so why did all these people pick him out for their personal relief?

'Of course you wouldn't think to look at me now' crooned the Welshman 'but at one time I was the best poacher around here for miles'...

'Really - how interesting!' said Rupert - as polite as he could -

'Yes really' glowered the Welshman - changing mood with the speed that only women and regular drunks can achieve -

'You taking the piss, bloody Sais eh? Sais... English you see!'

'No - not at all' placated Rupert - 'I mean these rural crafts are dying out aren't they?'

'Too bloody right they are' the Welshman said - coming close to Rupert and putting his arm round him 'You listen to me friend, I'll tell you - this bloody country has had it see - unless we get the bloody English out - isn't it?' His blood-shot eyes glared at Rupert - then a semblance of a smile crossed his face - 'Present company excepted of course - but you know what I mean....'

'No' uttered Rupert and he really didn't.

'Well look' said the now sober - now drunk Welshman... 'Look - who was it tried to stop the Welsh from having their own language eh? The bloody English!' He didn't wait for an answer from Rupert... 'Who was it claimed all the water rights eh? - the bloody English!' At this point he started to bang the counter -

A voice from the crowd at the tables called out -

'And who beat Wales at the Park on Saturday eh?'

There was a chorus of 'The bloody English!'

'And who had backed England to win and is still spending the money?' another caller from the pack -

'Bloody Dai Bottle' shouted the chorus -

Rupert's Welshman turned on the crowd,

'All right - but you mark my words - when we take over - then you'll see...' He spotted a pretty looking girl sitting among the crowd and weaved his way over to her - 'Hallo Shirley love, ain't I right then?' He plonked himself down beside her - having forgotten Rupert's existence.

Rupert swallowed the last of his pint and was all for getting to his room for a quiet watch of the English T.V. programmes, when a smart looking youngish to middle-aged dark-suited, balding and small man approached him.

Oh no - not again - thought Rupert and started to turn for the door - 'Excuse me' said the man - and although the accent was Welsh it was very slight, slight enough thought Rupert to be almost English.

'Would you allow me to buy you a drink - just to sort of make up for old Dai?' Rupert hesitated and was - of course - lost!

'Oh well - that's very kind of you - yes I'll have a lager - thank you'... At least this one seemed civilised.

'The name is Ianto - Ianto Price - I'm the local solicitor - well I will be when I qualify - but I still do the work..'

'Rupert Morgan' said Rupert, for some reason dropping the hyphenated Courtney -

'I understand that you are looking for some sort of property round here' - Rupert stared at the little man!

'Well' he stuttered -

'Oh - don't worry - the barman told me earlier - I was going to introduce myself but you were locked into the Second World War - Tobruk I think...'

He laughed as the fresh drinks appeared...

'Oh yes' said Rupert - 'That's right - amazing man really, when you think how many theatres of war he was in, isn't he?'

'Between you and me, Rupert,' said the solicitor - using Rupert's name as though he had known him since birth - which was a thing Rupert hated, but he said nothing - at least this chap did not say 'You don't mind if I call you Rupert do you?' - as some of them did - which was the silliest question in Rupert's opinion - and he always wanted to answer 'Yes I would rather you called me Arthur' - but never did...

'You don't mind if I call you Rupert - do you?'

'Not at all' said Rupert 'After all it is my name!' He laughed lightly - the solicitor didn't!

'Oh yes - quite - well Rupert, between you and me, I think most of the Brig's stories come from the Theatre - or rather the cinema - you know what I mean?'

'Yes I do see what you mean' said Rupert 'Pity though - he seems genuine doesn't he?'

The solicitor drank some of his drink - then quietly said

'A lot of things look genuine enough at first glance - but on closer scrutiny - well...' He looked at Rupert as though expecting some reply.

'Um' said Rupert 'That's very true...'

'Take you - for instance' smiled the solicitor 'You say you are looking for a property for a friend...'

'That's right' said Rupert hastily 'for a friend in London actually...'

'Ah!' sighed the little lawyer, 'Ah yes, for a friend - but I know different...'

Rupert was worried - had this man seen through his cover… The solicitor went on - 'It's like a friend of mine - newsagent he is - sells the strong stuff you know - Whitehouse - that sort of thing...' Rupert was used to being puzzled but this was a classic.

'No - I don't actually' he said -

'You know - of course you do' urged the mini Perry Mason…'Porno mags, nudy books...'

'Oh that ', said Rupert - disappointed - 'the Soho stuff'

'You've got it' said the solicitor -

'What about it?' asked Rupert - who had lost the thread of the story.

'Well my friend always says' - the little fellow leaned in to Rupert - 'That no-one buys a copy of these mags for himself - always for a friend see?'

Rupert wondered what the hell this little man was going on about... it had been a hard evening so far and he was well ready for bed...

'Ah yes, I see' said Rupert sipping his lager...

'So' - said the solicitor - 'This is what I am getting at - you are looking for property - I happen to know someone who can guide you to the best chances in this area - so I will introduce you...'

Oh why - thought Rupert - hadn't he just said he was on holiday? This well-meaning law man was going to complicate his life and hamper his investigations - he contemplated a law suit against the publishers of Bond as he turned to the gnomic pleader -

'That is most kind of you, but I am only looking around in a general sort of way - you know...' he hoped he sounded cool and a little dismissive - no chance -

'Excellent - then I have just the thing for you here'

The solicitor reached into his pocket and pulled out a tatty looking card which he handed Rupert - 'My card - sorry it's the only one I have at the moment - I am having some more printed but I am waiting until I have the letters you see..'

'Of course' said Rupert -

'Call in and see me tomorrow' said the unqualified solicitor - 'Anytime!'

'Thank you' said Rupert - making a mental note not to - 'I have one or two things to do, but I will try...'

'Good, good' said the bald councillor, 'I look forward to seeing you then.'

'Yes' said Rupert and made his way to the door 'Thank you - good night now'

'Goodnight' called Ianto Price watching Rupert very carefully as he left... 'Goodnight Englishman, sleep well', he whispered almost to himself... 'Sleep well!'

It was probably a good thing that Rupert could not see the look he gave the barman at that moment, it boded no good for innocent Englishmen abroad; and not much good for the barman either, as the little solicitor who had been steadily drinking all day, suddenly keeled over to his left and fell to the floor. No-one in the bar took much notice, and the barman just sighed and said 'I'll ring his wife!' to no-one in particular.

4   In Need of Slight Renovation Sir…

Rupert felt almost warm. The wind had not returned, the rain had stopped completely - but the moon was flirting with a few clouds and any moment threatened to expose herself totally. Rupert looked up and inspiration born of sheer terror hit him - it was a very big oak tree, with branches stretching out from a central bowl about eight feet up, but there were branches, small ones lower down so that he could - he thought - climb up into the bowl and be completely hidden from even the brightest moon - if he discarded his light coat... He took it off and rolled it into a ball and hoping no-one at that moment was actually looking directly at him - he threw the coat as far as he could towards a ditch some twenty to thirty feet off.... As luck would have it, the coat flew like a well thrown cricket ball - actually hit the hedge and spread itself out for all the world as though Rupert were still inside it.

Rupert stood dead still for a moment or two - nothing happened - so very quickly he reached up above his head and grabbed the nearest branch and with some effort managed to pull himself up into the bowl and crouch down. He felt fractionally safer - it had been good enough for a king - maybe it would work for him...

He remembered waking that first morning in Brecon, cramped in the single bed that was at least warm, as his room was directly above the kitchens - which seemed to hum with activity all through the night - scampering and scraping activity - small night shift waitresses no doubt! He had been told that many famous people in history had at one time or another stayed in this hotel; judging by the general air of must and decay some of them were still in residence. Breakfast, however, had been surprisingly good - bacon and egg and sausage, toast and butter, coffee and cream. The transport cafe was not far from the hotel and they had been very sincere in the hotel dining room - the breakfast chef was not well and as he was the only resident that night he could have just tea and maybe a biscuit... But he was hungry - and they had given him excellent directions... he had found it on only the second attempt.

He lingered over another coffee, as he planned his day - first he would make contact with the police Inspector - then maybe a trip up to where the accident or suicide or... whatever, had taken place - this worried Rupert as he had never had any dealings with death - apart from when his mother's pet budgie Byron - who understood every word mother said - had dropped dead in his cage, and after an hour Rupert had been asked by his mother to bury the body 'with reverence Rupert dear'...

All things considered, though, Rupert felt happy, he determined to conduct himself a little more like Bond and a little less like an ageing Adrian Mole - and consoled himself with the knowledge that this was his very first assignment - and with the cliché, that we all have to learn sometime...

The police station was not hard to find, once he had found a parking place for his car. It was market day in Brecon and it was crowded - even by the time that Rupert had got back to the town - which was about eleven o'clock. He walked into the station and approached the enquiry desk, behind which was standing a tall, thin, spotty faced police cadet - who was engrossed in a magazine of dubious literary content but high quality photography... Rupert waited for a few seconds before disturbing the enraptured embryo policeman then - 'Er... excuse me?'

The effect was electric, in as much as the cadet was shocked, therefore jumped sideways, closed the magazine, checked his flies, adjusted his tie, glared at Rupert, and pulled out a pen - all within the space of a very few heart beats.... and very calmly asked -

'Can I help you, sir?'

'Yes!' said Rupert, really very impressed with the young man's performance - 'I would like to see Inspector Thomas please.' The cadet looked at Rupert for a moment and then smiled -

'Which one sir?'

Rupert looked at the cadet, then pulled the letter of introduction from his pocket and having glanced at it said - 'Inspector D. T. Thomas, please' -

'Ah' - the cadet consulted a chart - out of Rupert's sight then said - 'D. T. Thomas - yes - well now what did you want to see the Inspector for?'

'It's about a death that took place here recently' said Rupert - taking out his official card and showing it to the young cadet - 'I work for the same firm as the man who - er - died....'

Rupert was about to continue, when a door behind the cadet opened and a large red-faced man - who looked like he could have been the brother of the drunk in the old boot hotel the night before, except for the fact that he was sober - stepped out and said to the cadet -

'If a young poofy blonde type idiot in a light coloured raincoat comes in asking for me Rogerson - I am on holiday - right!'

Cadet Rogerson, to his credit, did not scream, burst into hysterical laughter or faint, he simply turned to the Inspector and said - 'This is' - he looked carefully at the card he had been handed 'Mr Courtney Morgan from the

Department of Industrial Espionage, sir - he was just asking if he could see you - sir.'

The Inspector looked at Rupert, Rupert looked at the Inspector - the cadet looked at both of them - the tension built, like an episode from Dallas - the silence was total.

'Ah' - - the Inspector exhaled long and wheezily - 'Yes' on an 'in' breath - 'Ah' - 'out' breath 'Ah!'

'I have a letter from a Sergeant in Cardiff, here' - he handed the letter to the Inspector -

'Yes yes...' uttered the Inspector, taking the letter but not opening it... 'Yes, yes... funny department yours - isn't it'

Rupert looked at him, wondering if it was the drunk from last night...

'I mean' continued the Inspector, 'D.I.E.... I mean I have heard of D.I.Y., but D.I.E. - Do it yourself spying is it?' Rupert cringed, this was the old boring joke that was always cracked by sophisticated drunks in London - he never expected to find it here.

'Lot of nonsense if you ask me' carried on the Inspector 'Look - I know why you are here, to do with that unfortunate happening up on the bank now - well let me tell you Mr... er... Morgan... there is no doubt that it was suicide - a bit strange and weird perhaps - but suicide never the less. Now I know that you London types imagine that we who work out in the country areas are not up to your high quality, but we know a thing or two Mr...' he checked the card again 'Morgan... oh yes!'

Rupert stared at him not sure of what to say. 'I'm not sure what to say, Inspector, I didn't mean to infer any criticism of your force - I have been sent down by my Department - simply to find out what happened and report back - that's all... I mean...' The Inspector glared at him then turning on his heel, he skidded into the door post and would have fallen if the cadet had not steadied him.

'Bloody cleaners - they do it deliberately...' he scuffed the floor as though to get revenge... 'Come into my office Mr... er... Morgan.' He led the way - walking very carefully on the Torville and Dean floor - Rupert followed, glad that he was wearing his man-made soles today..

They entered a small but compact office. The Inspector told him to sit down - there was only one chair and a small empty table, Rupert sat in the chair - the Inspector sat on the edge of the table leaning over Rupert slightly. It was vaguely like the scenes from an old Bogart film, except there should have been a spot lamp.

'I should by rights have a spotlight in here' laughed the Inspector - 'Sorry' - he went on 'Just a joke - my office is being redecorated you see, so I use this one for interviews... Now about this little affair..'

'Ah yes - a mere matter of a death' said Rupert, who was beginning to dislike this policeman -

'People die every day, Mr Morgan, it just so happens that this one happened here - and there were a few odd circumstances - not that any death is ordinary to those who do the dying, is it - but the local man in Cardiff was quite satisfied with the report from my station - why are you really here Mr Morgan?'

'I am here because my boss in London told me to come here, Inspector - and I never said that anything was wrong - did I?'

'No you didn't' - the Inspector got off the table and walked around the room. 'No you didn't' he repeated 'but I can't see why you should be here unless you think that you are capable of finding out more than us poor country Bobbies. It's always the same... every spy book you read some suave London bastard comes swarming down to the sticks, and straight away the simplest of traffic offences is tied up with the sodding Russians - taking control of the red traffic lights and causing havoc - killing agents -' His voice rose an octave - 'The idiot local copper keeps apologizing and saying 'I had no idea sir - it seemed straightforward to me'... your suave Bond just smiles cynically - sinks another ten vodkas - swims two miles underwater - screws five page three birds - blows up half the native population - and then gets offered a bloody knighthood - which he refuses... because saving the sodding world is just part of his daily routine..' The Inspector whirled on Rupert -

'Well let me tell you Mr bloody secret sodding agent Morgan - or whatever your name is, most of you London types couldn't tell a case of attempted rape from a drunk driving charge - let alone save the world - so there... Your friend drove up the bloody mountain - stuck the bloody tube in his mouth - turned on the engine and topped himself - end of story - we went and picked him up and cleaned up the mess - that's all!'

Rupert studied the Inspector for a few moments - something about this case was definitely not right - everyone he had met so far went crazy at the mention of the death of Blanchard.... Deep down inside of course, he agreed with the Inspector - the spy books did tend to make it seem very easy - the hero always seemed to be in the right vicinity at the right time when things began to happen - but Rupert supposed that it did save time - after all if the fate of the world was held in the balance on a remote island in the south China seas by a mad Polish dwarf with a grievance against six foot heterosexual negroes - it would not be a very gripping novel if the hero was following a lead in a drinking club in Bromley South.

The cadet popped his head round the door and looked worried - 'Everything all right sir?'

'Yes, yes -' The Inspector walked over to the door - 'yes - yes - just bring us some tea will you - oh and the file on that suicide - ' he glared at Rupert - the cadet nodded and left the room... 'All I can do for you Mr Morgan is let you see the file and give you directions to the site of the incident - after that - if you have your magnifying glass with you and your multi-channel radio lighter and whatever other equipment you types carry around - you can play detective till kingdom come for all I care!'

The door opened again - the cadet entered and handed a file to the Inspector - and put two plastic cups down on the table - steam rose from the cups... The cadet left without saying anything - the Inspector took one of the cups and pushed the other toward Rupert along with the file - then turned his back and stared out of the window... Rupert glanced at the tea - decided that he was not thirsty, and opened the file. There was only one page of writing stating the very barest of bare facts - and a note at the bottom to the effect that the body was being held in the Police Morgue in Cardiff...

'Is this all there is?' asked Rupert - aware that in his department the request for a new typewriter ribbon would have created far more paperwork...

'It's all there need be' growled the Inspector, 'what more do you want - a bloody novel on 'how I found a body on the Beacons' 'Death on the Hillside by D.T. Thomas' - that what you want eh? Well you've had it son - that's the report - like it or leave it.... if you see that spotty faced cadet on your way out you will get the directions to the killing ground' - he laughed nastily -

Rupert went to the door - paused and turned - looked at the Inspector - 'How much did you have on England to win?' he asked -

'Twenty bloody quid - ' the Inspector stopped - glared at Rupert in bewilderment -

'How did you...? '

Rupert just smiled and went out.

'Clever bastard!' muttered the Inspector....

The cadet had drawn a sketch map of how to reach the spot where Blanchard had died - he handed it to Rupert - 'There are a couple of houses just before you turn off here' he indicated a place on the sketch - 'If you are not sure - ask at one of them' -

'Thank you' - Rupert tucked the paper away in his pocket and was about to leave -

'Go carefully Mr Morgan' - the cadet said - 'The Beacons can be dangerous - specially at this time of year...' Rupert was about to say something but the cadet turned and went into a room behind the counter... Was he trying to warn him - thought Rupert - or was he just being helpful? At least he was getting to the start of the whole mess - he would have a look at the spot and then try and trace the movements of Blanchard to that point, but first he decided to have a cup of coffee.

He walked back to the Old Boot Hotel hoping that the breakfast chef was not in charge of coffees - he wandered into the lounge bar which was not quite deserted... for in the corner of the bar - sitting on a stool - hugging a coffee cup was - Ianto Price - the little bald solicitor. Rupert hoped for a second or two that he could beat a retreat - but was stopped by the little man who had obviously been waiting for him...

'Ah - I have been waiting for you, Mr Morgan - didn't I say I would meet you here at eleven?'

'No' replied Rupert - who was quite sure that he had not made any such plans.

'Yes, yes' - the solicitor reached into his pocket and pulled out a piece of paper - 'Said I had a property - didn't I... well here you are - just what you... ha... your friend could be looking for... super spot... complete isolation... no noisy neighbours... here!' He thrust the paper at Rupert who had no choice but to take it and he realised that it was important to keep his cover intact...

'Oh yes - how silly of me - it must be the country air - made me sleepy last night - I remember now -' He looked at the paper in front of him - it showed a derelict looking farmhouse surrounded by trees that looked as though they had been pruned with a blunt chainsaw. He couldn't see much as it was a very bad photocopy of what had never been a good picture to start with - he started to read through the blurb....

'No need to read through all that guff' said the little lawyer - 'Most of it's rubbish for the ordinary punter - but I can tell you that this is a snip - only just come on the market - of course it has been empty for some time - but well - a coat of paint and a few bits of wood - that sort of thing you know...'

'What happened to the trees?' asked Rupert -

'Vandals' - the solicitor said without hesitation 'Vandals you know how it is around Christmas - after the trees. Needs a good owner - been empty too long - look, don't let me press you or anything - but you can take my word for it - this is a bargain - why don't you go and have a look at it - today - while the weather holds eh? - Good! Look I have drawn a map of how to get there - on the back.'

Rupert turned the paper over, and on the back was a sketch that almost matched the one he had been given by the police cadet.... Well - it was odd - but at the same time - it was useful - for he could go to the house and look at the 'killing ground' without arousing any suspicion...

'That's very kind of you Mr Price, very kind, thank you - I will go up there I think - just have a look around - you know...'

Rupert turned for the door - he had given up all hope of anyone coming to take his order for coffee -

'Good - good' cried the lawman - 'But don't forget I did say it was in need of slight renovation - won't you?'

Rupert thanked him again - and left. The solicitor turned and faced the bar - his face tense with concentration - at last he seemed to make up his mind and reaching over the bar took the bell and rang it....The barman appeared -

'Large gin and tonic' ordered the advocate with the full authority of the law behind him.

5   Home on the range

The wind had returned, cramp had arrived, Rupert felt like a block of ice in a pub ice-making machine - any moment he expected to be blown through the branches of his sanctuary and scattered across the countryside in drink size pieces. He eased his arms and legs as best he could and thought back to the place where Blanchard had died.

It was while he was standing at the spot where Blanchard's car had been found that Rupert began to suspect that there was more to the agent's death than he was being told - for why should anyone - even someone depressed enough to want to commit suicide - drive to such a god-forsaken spot as this. To Rupert it was like a scene shot after the bomb had dropped on Hampstead Heath. There were trees - but they were hacked off at the base - and the grass was scorched. It occurred to Rupert that something evil had taken place here - apart from Blanchard's death - he searched the ground around the area where the car had been standing - but of course, found nothing - he decided that he had better visit the house the solicitor had told him about - just to keep his cover intact. He drove on into the desolation for about a mile before he saw the house...

Isolated - the man had said - Neil Armstrong had more neighbours on the moon landing than this. Rupert parked the car - in what would have been the front garden of any other house. He walked to the door - he pushed - the door opened swinging on one hinge for a second or two then crashed to the ground - - oh well - thought Rupert - it was after all meant to be a derelict - he entered - eerie, that was what it was - so very quiet and eerie. The first room was a sort of loungette - a small ante room leading to a larger reception area - green faded wallpaper lined the walls - grey cracked slate slabs were covering the floor - the air smelled of must, dust, old age, gunpowder...Gunpowder? - Rupert's mind was puzzled - all the other things he could understand - but why - gunpowder... As he was contemplating this strange smell a noise distracted him - a low screeching howling noise that ended in a familiar whump.... that he had heard so many times in John Wayne movies - shells... mortar shells!

The ground shook under him and he was thrown to the flagstone floor as another shell landed within inches of the house - or so it seemed to Rupert. He scrabbled across the floor on all fours towards a door that was a bit more substantial than the rest of the building - he pulled at the bottom of it - not daring to stand as more shells seemed to bracket the house - the door opened as though well-oiled and Rupert saw that there was a flight of stairs going down into the darkness.

As much afraid of the dark as he was - the lower level of this house seemed to offer some safety - so Rupert slithered forward and down the stairs in the pitch dark until he came to what felt like more flagstones. He lay there shaking as shell after shell exploded around the house.... his mind was in a turmoil... someone was trying to kill him.... that was obvious... but - to go to such lengths - mortar bombs! Just did not make sense... his enemies weren't that rich.... he slid across the floor of the basement trying to get as far away as possible from the noise - when he heard a voice quite close to his left ear -

'Cease fire red leader one - red leader one - do you read - cease fire' - A crackly voice answered 'Cease fire - Blue control - fire ceased' -

'Thank you red leader - target destroyed - over!' 'Hello blue control - target now destroyed - confirmed - thank you - your round tonight - Roger...'

'No chance red leader - over and out...' There was a short silence - then - 'put the bloody light on someone - the show's over...' There was a sharp click, and Rupert blinked as the room was flooded with florescent light, just to his left and above him - as he was still on the floor - sat two soldiers facing a radio console - opposite and standing by what seemed to be a submarine type periscope stood another soldier who had obviously been the one to turn on the lights - as he still had his hand on the switch as he saw Rupert squirming around on the floor -

'WHO THE F**K ARE YOU?' - he spoke quite pleasantly and quietly - Rupert struggled to his feet and stood with his back to the wall staring at the three soldiers - who in their turn, stared at him with something akin to stupefied amazement... Rupert cleared his throat, tried to speak, failed and then tried again....

'Are you the Welsh free army?' - he finally squeaked. The soldiers looked at him - then at each other – then the one who appeared to be the leader said -

'No mate - we're the English - highly expensive - army' - he smiled at Rupert 'But to repeat the Corporal's comment, sunshine, who the - joining together of male and female in the act of copulation leading to procreation - are you?? And while you are pondering on the answer to that question - here is another - how the repeat aforesaid statement as to the loving ritual - did you get here??'

Before Rupert could begin to answer - one of the other men spoke, 'Very good Sarge - wait till I tell the Padre' - he looked at Rupert - 'we have this Padre at camp see - and he is trying to improve the image of the British soldier singlehanded, so he awards points for any man who can think of any way of avoiding the common and offensive swear words favoured by your average squaddy... the Sarge here should warrant a few hundred bonus points for that comment, seeing as the circumstances would tempt the most contemplative of saints'... Rupert was completely lost -

'I am completely lost!'

The soldier by the periscope spoke up - 'Well, speaking for myself like - I don't go along with the Padre trying to change the formula that successfully beat Napoleon, the German Army twice and the Argies - so who the fuck are you and how the fuck did you get in here?'

'I was given this address as a possible country cottage for sale.'...

The Sergeant who was slowly winding up a coil of cable went up to Rupert - 'Son - I would change your estate agent - how did you get here - walk?'

'No I drove - my car is outside' -

'Have a look Pete' - this was to the soldier by the periscope, which he now raised - stuck his face into the eyepiece and slowly gyrated in the best U boat tradition - suddenly he stopped and reversed - - 'Ah' - he swung the 'scope round a bit further - then 'Ah - ah!' - then he swung right round - finally 'Ah!'

'Well Pete' said the Sergeant with great calmness - Pete swung up the handle of the periscope and lowered it down into a hole in the floor - he turned slowly -

'Well Sarge - I have good news and bad news - regarding this gentleman's car...' - nobody spoke - the other two soldiers were obviously used to Pete's manner and Rupert couldn't think of anything that would be of any value - Pete - seeing he had the floor - spoke - 'The good news is that your car, sir' - he looked at Rupert and smiled

- 'Your car, sir, is still out there' - He indicated the outside. 'The bad news is...' he paused - 'Are you any good at jigsaw puzzles?...'

Rupert gaped - The Sergeant spoke - 'A direct hit - .eh?'

'Right on the button Sarge' he smiled again - turned to Rupert 'Er - what was it in real life?'

'A mini metro' said Rupert - still not quite believing all this -

'Em - I didn't know there were so many pieces in a metro... still look at it this way - son - you could have been in it couldn't you?'

Rupert tried hard to pull himself together... 'Look - I am sorry - but could you please explain to me - in simple terms - just what is going on...'

The Sarge looked at him carefully 'Harry - this gentleman is in shock - break out the tea flask'

'Yes Sarge' said the third soldier - and he walked over to a pile of army type boxes on the floor...

'Sit down son' the Sergeant led Rupert to a chair near the radio - Rupert sat gratefully - 'Now then - let me explain first where you are' - the Sergeant pulled a map towards him and pointed to a spot in the centre... 'Here you are... target area Number four - top security - delayed mortar attack - today's date and time - see?'

Rupert saw and his mind was racing - 'Then this is a firing range of some kind then?'

The soldier called Harry came over with a mug of what looked like black steaming treacle - he plonked it down in front of Rupert.

'I bloody hope so mate - otherwise I would be very worried about the natives around here - letting off mortars and what not...' he laughed not unkindly and went back to his chair. . .'If you drove in son, you must have seen the notices - and the red flags - warning you where you were'

'I saw none at all' said Rupert - 'not one'...

'That is very strange' said the Sergeant, 'who told you about this house being for sale then?'

Rupert pulled out the piece of paper with the house details and handed it to the Sergeant - 'A solicitor in the town gave me this - and told me how to get here...'

'That the only person to tell you - was it?' The Sergeant sounded suspicious...

'Well yes - I said I was looking for property in the area and he came up with this - I had no idea…' he trailed off as the other two soldiers had moved up to the Sergeant and were looking at the paper... 'What was the name of this solicitor?' It was the soldier called Pete who asked the question.

'Er... Price I think... yes... Ianto Price...' Rupert had some trouble with the pronunciation of Ianto...

There was a long pause - then - 'How long have you known this Ianto Price?'

'I don't know him, he came up to me in a bar last night... we talked and he said he could help me...' even to Rupert it sounded fatuous.... The Sergeant walked around to the periscope and pulled it up and looked through it - and while he was looking - 'What's your name son?'

'Rupert Courtney Morgan' - the tone of the Sergeant's voice almost brought forth a 'sir' from Rupert... 'You often get strange men coming up to you in bars do you?' The question seemed innocent enough, but Rupert could sense a certain undercurrent that was familiar to him... 'No I don't... well that is I didn't - not until I came down to Wales....'

'And just what brought you down to Wales then?' This question from the one called Pete - 'I told you I was looking for...' he didn't finish - 'Come off it Rupert...' the way the Sergeant used his name sent a shiver down his back... 'I know' continued the Sergeant 'that there is a certain anti-English feeling among the less intelligent of Welsh people - but even they usually confine their dislike to insults in Welsh or at worst burning down some isolated holiday cottage - just to prove that they can afford a gallon of petrol... but on the whole the rational Welsh people realize that money is money whether it is English or bloody Russian... they moan a lot - they shout a lot - they drink a lot - but what they do not do is deliberately set someone up to be blown to kingdom come because he expresses a desire to buy a Welsh farm house... and - if they did - they would at least make sure they had the money first... so Rupert Mate - what are you really doing here eh?'

Rupert realised that he would have to tell these men, and after all - they were English... He reached into his inside pocket but before his arm had travelled far it was pinned to his chest by the soldier called Harry - 'Careful Rupert' - Harry whispered - 'Very careful...'

Rupert's hand felt the card case and he removed it holding it up high to show them that it was harmless... then he extracted a card and handed it to the Sergeant - who took it carefully and held it under the light - he read it slowly... then turned to Rupert -

'Someone been stealing a new beef burger formula then?'

'No - not exactly'....

The Sergeant looked at the card again and then back to Rupert... 'Look son, I don't know much about these civilian outfits, but on the whole I imagine that they do not go in for the James Bond type stuff - so what is really going on here?'

Rupert stared at the Sergeant, 'Sergeant - I really wish I knew' - Rupert tried to drink some of the tea he had been given - it was a mistake - he coughed then slowly the room seemed to dissolve.... the three soldiers just disappeared... the last thing he was aware of was the Sergeant speaking 'I hope you haven't overdone it Pete, that stuff can be lethal! '

'No - Sarge - I only put a drop in. Do you think he's one of them then Sarge?'

'Difficult to say nowadays - isn't it - let's say if he isn't then he looks it...'

There was a sound like the wild screaming of a demented egg whisk and Rupert knew no more - for the time being....

6   It's a Man's Life

The scream of the owl two inches from Rupert's left ear woke him! Apart from the pain of stiff arms and legs, the most amazing thing to Rupert was that he had actually fallen asleep in the tree. He looked around as far as his position would allow him and he listened... He could see and hear nothing... well nothing human... He relaxed a little, and remembered the last strange awakening he had experienced...

It was black inside the tube, pitch black, there was no sound - Rupert seemed to be walking forwards and despite the dark he was walking quite confidently - the ground was firm under his feet, he could not feel the sides of the tube yet he knew it was a tube - then he knew it was a tunnel... ahead of him he suddenly saw floating at about head height a green florescent rugby ball, it was turning on its axis as it floated towards him... He tried to remember how he was supposed to catch it - he knew he must not throw it forwards...

It came nearer and he reached out - his hands ready to take it when it suddenly changed and was the head of Iestyn Morris from the Cardiff Branch of D.I.E.- the head turned towards him and spoke - 'Don't mention the wig will you boyo... Head Office only likes hairy heads... Please don't mention the wig, please....' The voice trailed off in a long whine, coupled with sobs of despair.

Rupert walked on as though the head was a normal occurrence, next he became aware of a field stretching as far as he could see - he turned to check where the tunnel was that he had emerged from - but in every direction there was just field - which way shall I go, he asked himself... a voice from outside 'Why Don't you ask Megan' - he whirled around and sat at the dining table that was fully laid for breakfast... The waitress was standing, bored...

'What did you say' asked Rupert -

'Do you want black or white laver bread?'

A black mass of thick goo clamped itself over Rupert's eyes - he screamed and clawed at his face -

'He's coming round Sarge' - a normal voice from above spoke quietly - Rupert opened his eyes - he was lying on a cot like bed, the ceiling above him was curved away like a large tube, he could feel movement, vibration... a strange sense of floating - yet not floating... He lifted his head - at the bottom of the bed was the soldier called Pete - he was replacing the face mask of an oxygen pack back on to a tall cylinder - he looked towards Rupert.

'Hello - you feeling all right now? Gave us a bit of a shock - you keeling over like that you know...' Rupert shook his head - trying to remember how he got here...'What happened.... where am I?' he said, thinking incongruously that that was probably the most used phrase in all thrillers - 'What happened - where am I?' he said again..

'Why did you say that twice?' asked Pete the soldier

'I don't know' said Rupert 'It just struck me that it must be a very much used phrase... you know...'

Pete stared a moment at Rupert - then 'Well yes I suppose it is - but in this case the answer may be a little less used...'

'What is the answer?' Rupert thought he ought to ask -

'Simple' - Pete pulled a curtain aside from a window - Rupert saw that it was a round window - more like a port hole - then he became aware of a steady throbbing hum - a regular vibration - Pete watched him, smiling -

'That's right Rupert - it's an aeroplane - an R.A.F. Hercules to be exact - flying at about two thousand feet - heading for R.A.F. Brawdy in South Wales. What happened was that, after suffering a severe shock - your car was blown out of existence, by accident of course, during an army exercise - you fainted - so we are taking you to a military hospital for a check-up...

'But I didn't faint' - said Rupert - who was vaguely remembering the tea - and the strange taste -

'As far as it matters - you did' said Pete not unkindly - Rupert lay back on the bed, totally confused - what had all this to do with his simple investigation... He looked up - Pete was offering him a cigarette - he took it gratefully - felt in his pocket for his lighter - then realised that he was not wearing his clothes but was dressed in plain pyjamas....

'Where?' he started...

'Don't worry' Pete answered, 'They are safe...we had to have you examined properly didn't we... here - ' he leaned forward and lit Rupert's cigarette...

Apart from a few bumps and alarming type lurches, the flight was uneventful. Rupert spent the time trying to make some kind of sense from all his experiences so far in Wales - he failed!

Blanchard - a Cardiff based operative for the department had been found dead.... he was not on any kind of mission, it was not that kind of job - the people who Rupert had spoken to so far had all told him that Blanchard was gay - well, so what, there was a lot of that sort of thing about nowadays... they even had their very own groups - gay lib - Gay News and what not.... it was not in itself a reason for dying on a Welsh mountain... Both the policemen he had spoken to were emphatic that Blanchard had killed himself - perhaps they were too emphatic? Then there was the solicitor.... he must have known that the house he sent Rupert to see was on the army firing range... but most strange of all was that he found that he liked the taste of laver bread and was beginning to get a craving for the black stuff.

As soon as the plane had landed Rupert was carried on the same bed to a waiting ambulance - which took off at speed - Rupert could not see out of the windows so had no idea which way he was heading.... After what seemed about twenty minutes the ambulance stopped and Rupert was carried out and into a low clean looking building...

'You can get out of the bed now, Morgan!' Rupert sat up with a jerk... sitting in a chair at the foot of the bed, stroking a large black cat, but now wearing a pin-striped suit was the Head of the Department.... 'Well Morgan, you have been having some fun haven't you?' Rupert just stared at the Boss - was he being funny - was he serious - was he just mad - did he expect an answer... 'Yes sir' said Rupert - then quickly 'If you say so, sir, but frankly I don't think it was all that enjoyable, sir'. The Chief stroked the cat for a moment or two, then stood up and went to look out of the window....

'You don't like the work - eh Morgan...'

'What?' said Rupert, wishing he hadn't. 'I mean - no well yes, really it's just that I was not expecting - well - you know sir - most of the time when I go to the lectures - my normal work - the people sit quietly bored I mean - they don't try to kill me - if you see what I mean, sir...' Rupert lapsed into silence - now wishing he had stopped at 'what?'....

The Chief eyed him, walked round him, then clicked something inside the cat, turning again to Rupert he said... 'Well done, Morgan, I knew you were the man for the job... I just wanted to make sure...' - Rupert gaped... But before he could speak the door opened and in came Miss Romanov - carrying a pink file - looked at Rupert - winked her special kind of wink - handed the file to the Chief and went out again. Rupert wondered vaguely if there was more to the relationship between her and the Chief than her just being his secretary...

'She is also my chauffeur Morgan - in case you are wondering...'

'Oh - er - no - I mean...'

'It means I can stay on the job while I am travelling you see?'

'Oh, yes of course' - Rupert decided that if there was a course on how to act and sound confident advertised in the next Sunday Times supplement he was going to write off and enrol.... 'Now' - the Chief was talking again... 'In this file is your new identity...' He opened the file and handed Rupert a photo - it looked like Rupert but with subtle differences....

'But sir!' Rupert started to complain...

'I know' said the Chief quickly 'It makes you look like a dark haired member of the gay fraternity - but that is exactly what it is supposed to do - you are going into the arts - Morgan!' Rupert was beginning to think he could enter for the world 'gaping and saying er - I - well - what' record...

'Er, I - well - what sir?'

'But first you are going to join the Army!' Rupert stayed with the previous gape - it did not seem worthwhile to start a new one...

'Yes sir' was all he said...

'Yes Morgan, this case has taken on a more serious nature since you were first briefed - I'm sorry that we could not contact you in time to warn you - but as it happens - it has turned out for the best... since you are now officially dead!' Rupert shut his mouth and stopped gaping - as a mark of respect for the dead... and thought that his parents were going to be upset

'Dead sir...?'

'Yes, as far as the world is concerned, you were still in your car when a stray mortar hit it... most regrettable... but there you are... or were... you shouldn't have been there anyway.... no body of course... all very nasty... next of kin have been informed....'

Rupert felt most strange - like being an orphan in reverse... He didn't like it much.... but then realised that it was only for a while then he could go and tell his parents all was well - and - that they were not a childless couple any more - that made him feel better.

'For the purpose of your new identity Morgan, you are being seconded to the Army Pay Corp - Rank of Sergeant, Entertainment Detail... give you some background of the arts... but of course you will not be going anywhere near their headquarters or barracks - no - you have been transferred to the Special Investigation Branch of Counter Espionage - known as Central External Surveillance Section... Sub Section P/OO/L - who have kindly lent you to us for the duration of the investigation - so in effect you will be working directly under my control - it makes life a lot easier.'

'Yes sir...' Rupert's brain was still struggling with the fact that his parents were probably at this moment thinking of letting his room - which they always kept at home in case he ever decided to go back....

'What is my name, sir?' he said, suddenly becoming aware of what in fact was going on.... 'I mean I won't be able to use my real one - will I?'

'Certainly not Morgan.... not at all and you must get used to your new one quickly - you must answer to it as though you have always been called it...'

'But what is it sir?'

'What? Haven't I told you?'

'No sir!'

'Um... most remiss'. He dived into the file and pulled out a sheet of paper - he consulted it for a moment - then smiled... 'Um - yes well - it will do' he looked at Rupert... 'Vivian... Vivian P Williams...'

'Vivian, but that's a....'

'Not spelt this way... and besides we want you to appear a bit, how shall we say - ambiguous... right?'

'Yes sir' - the day was altogether too confusing...

'Now the first thing you have to do is memorise this short history of your life, then I am sending you for a short training course on unarmed combat - weapon training - that sort of thing...'

For the first time in a long while Rupert's spirits rose - this was more like it - he was to become a real agent - a highly trained fighting machine... The Chief was still talking

'The men who are in the know tell me that these gays can be very vicious if aroused - so you will be taught all the tricks - how to avoid having your hair pulled - keeping your knees together - that sort of thing..'

'What about guns sir?' Rupert's spirits were on the descent again...

'Good god Morgan... ah Williams... guns... no way - you might kill someone - no, no guns Morgan - Williams - you will have to use your wits and whatever you pick up in training... and of course the weight of the Department will be right behind you - I will see to it that there is a cover agent somewhere around at all times of likely danger..'

Rupert wanted to say 'No sir - if you remember I always prefer to work alone - and this is no exception - no cover or the deal's off....'

'Only one sir? I mean I could be moving about quite a lot and supposing my cover lost me...'

'Sorry Morgan, Williams - this is not the C.I.A. you know! Now I must go - I have an appointment in London. Good luck Mor... Williams... we are depending on you.' With that short speech the Chief opened the window - stepped over the sill - just as a large black car pulled up outside. He stepped into it and was whisked away.

Rupert sat on the bed trying to pull all the ends of this strange day together. The door opened - a large red-faced man in army khaki entered - stared at Rupert in absolute disgust...

'Sarnt. Williams. .. Sarnt... Vivian Williams… Pay Corp is it?'

Rupert leapt to his feet and to attention and snapped off a 'yes sir' before he had even had time to think...

'Follow me Sergeant, and try to look like a bloody soldier... my god and they say it's a man's life in the British Army...'

Rupert stumbled after the Sergeant, finding it very difficult to march smartly in pyjamas with no cord.

7 Beware the Gifts Bearing Leeks

Rupert shifted his position again and tried to guess the time - how long had he been in the tree - surely the men would have given up by now. There were a lot of fields and woods around - there was no way surely that they would track him down to this tree. But then he thought of his briefing just before he was let loose for the second time on his mission... perhaps they would not give up after all.

The room looked dusty in the bright cold sunlight of the October morning. From outside could be heard the sound of students shouting, running, happily playing in the quad, throwing eggs - in practise for a visiting lecturer from the Government. Inside, sitting across from Rupert at a normal office type desk sat Professor Brewster Goronwy ap Hazarde - one of the greatest authorities on the Welsh nation and history. A dry, dusty little man but with very pale blue, piercing eyes that darted this way and that as though searching the very crevices of the walls for more knowledge on his beloved Wales - as he always called it - his long white hair, flowed down from his high balding head and rested on his dandruff flecked shoulders, his small hands played restlessly with a black, burned, long stemmed, unlit pipe. Finally his eyes came to rest on Rupert.

'Know much about Welsh history, do you then?' His voice was high pitched and slightly musical - in that it went up and down like some ancient prehistoric scale.

'No - absolutely nothing' said Rupert - although this was not strictly true, he had, for instance, heard of Dylan Thomas, Max Boyce, Harry Secombe, Rhys ap Thomas and Barry John... and he knew that the Prince of Wales was directly - or was it obliquely - connected to Owen

Glyndwr - who was also Prince of Wales. But he had been told - Rupert that is - that he should pretend to total ignorance in front of this venerable Professor...

'Good' - piped the said Professor - 'I can't stand anyone who pretends to knowledge that they don't have. Well a short history is called for, I think, as many of you English never take the time to find out the facts about other nations and believe me Mr... er...' - he looked down at a paper in front of him - 'Mr Williams - believe me - there is more to the Welsh Nation than Harry Secombe, Max Boyce, Barry John and Dylan Thomas... there is for instance Rhys ap Thomas and Owen Glyndwr - oh yes, yes!' He paused and took out a box of matches - struck one and attempted to light his pipe, sucking at it and talking at the same time in a way pipe smokers do when they want to sound reflective and intelligent...

'But' - suck - 'even more than them' - suck - 'there are the druids you know' - strike suck, suck, suck - 'the druids... yes, yes... very old... pre-Christian culture you know' - suck, suck - ignition... clouds of smoke rose around the face of the Professor from out of which came... 'But of course that far back is of no use to you, in your present condition...'

Rupert tried to think what the Professor meant by condition... 'I mean' continued the old boy, 'you are interested in the more modern history, even more particularly the growth of the modern epidemic of the' - he stopped suddenly, coughed, slumped forward, coughed again, looked up - put the pipe down in an ash tray on the desk - took out a handkerchief and wiped his eyes as he coughed once more - sat back in his chair breathing heavily...

'Are you all right?' asked Rupert, who was sure that the old man was about to expire from a heart attack...

'Oh yes, yes I am fine...' he wheezed 'it's the tobacco - the wife puts some grass cuttings and weeds in it - she is trying to stop me smoking'... He coughed once more - then - 'I am sorry - where was I?'

'You were about to tell about the modern epidemic of something...'

'Oh yes...' the Professor got out of his chair, moved around to the door, opened it - looked out - shut it carefully, came back to his desk - sat - looked at Rupert -

'Have you ever heard of the 'Tafia`?'

'Do you mean the Mafia?' said Rupert thinking that he had misheard the question -

'No I do not mean the Mafia' - humphed the Professor - 'I said the Tafia and I meant the Tafia!' He stared at Rupert as though trying to read his mind... 'You probably think it is some kind of joke eh?'

'No!' said Rupert hurriedly - though he did think it was a little funny -

'Well let me tell you Mr Williams... the Tafia are no joke - no indeed - they are an organisation, much older than the so-called Mafioso of Corsica - in fact in my opinion - and I am, as you know, one of the foremost authorities on Welsh History - it is my opinion that the Corsican Mafia is in fact - an off-shoot of the Tafia... as indeed we all know that as the Welsh language predates the English... so does the rule of the families of Ogmore..'

Rupert sat back, willing to listen to the expert, and with any luck he might find a clue to his mission. The Professor fingered his pipe for a moment - then thought better of it and continued...

'To understand the Tafia properly we have to go back to the Dark Ages - the times when the Welsh Tribes wandered unhindered in the valleys and mountains, before the coming of the Tyrants of Rome, England and France.

Many tribes there were, scattered all over the country, and because of the rugged and difficult terrain - they were on the whole largely unaware of each other's existence - therefore, naturally, they each thought of themselves as the true natives of the country in which they lived... that is until the outsiders came - opening up roads - letting in the knowledge of the other tribes...' he paused as though seeing it all as it was....

'Ah Mr Williams bach, can you imagine the shock... for centuries you were safe in the knowledge that you were the chosen race of God... then in come these heathens with tales of many other tribes... the cultural shock must have been enormous... do you see?'

'Oh yes, quite...' said Rupert 'It must have been awful for them.'

The Professor looked at Rupert with his most piercing look, then deciding that Rupert was not trying to be funny continued - 'Yes indeed, but of course, worse than just opening up the world to the tribes, the outsiders, in the manner of all outsiders, wanted to rule the people as well - take them as slaves - that sort of thing - well naturally the Welsh did not like this - but as they were scattered all over the place they could never get together in sufficient numbers to make a decent fight of it - see?'

Rupert nodded and grunted his agreement in an intelligent manner -

'That was until the coming of Ogmore the First of Gwent - a great man Mr Williams - a great man indeed - the first man to find a way of defeating the outsiders without the outsiders knowing that they were being defeated see?'

Rupert nodded again - though this time he was completely lost...

'Brilliant he was' - the Professor was glowing with inner enthusiasm now - 'Brilliant - he started the Tafia way back in the dark mists of time and now it is stronger than ever... and still runs on much the same lines as then - only now of course the intentions are very different. In the first days it was there to protect and help the peasants against the invaders - now it is the machine of the ambitious men - greedy men Mr Williams - greedy for power and ..' He stopped, stared at the ceiling as though trying to hold back deep emotion...

'But how does it work?' asked Rupert, who was totally confused. The Professor brought his eyes down from the ceiling and focussed on Rupert -

'Mr Williams, what I am about to tell you is the result of many years of research and study - I have not told anyone the whole of my findings - as most people would think I was quite mad... but believe me... I know...' He stood up, went over to the door again, opened it, stared out, shut it, came back and stood in front of the window looking out over the quad.

'You will not be able to stop them Mr Williams - no-one can, but if you can only let the world know of their existence then, maybe one day...' - he tailed off... and turned back to Rupert. 'I am sorry - you want facts that you can work on - yes, yes - I get carried away you know '

Rupert thought that the old fool should be carried away; he wanted to scream at him 'What do they do for Christ sake?' but he just smiled and nodded at the Professor and hoped that he would tell him something useful before lunch time…

'They are everywhere Mr Williams, everywhere, they have infiltrated into every walk of life... How? I hear you say - Ah! Now there is the clever thing... Ogmore's Plank... Ogmore's Plank....' He smiled to himself - 'My name for it, of course - like Morton's Fork - Ogmore's Plank!'

'Ogmore's Plank?' repeated Rupert - 'what was it then?'

'Then?' The Professor laughed... 'Then? - Now, boy, now - all around you, and I discovered it, yes!' He stopped and smiled at Rupert...'I am sorry my boy, but you see, no-one knows of it yet, and you are the first, so forgive my indulgence. Now seriously - Ogmore's Plank! Ogmore was a little man by all accounts, little - but very bright. When he saw the invaders taking over life everywhere and the people being killed if they dared to object, he, being one of nature's cowards, thought up his idea. Why not - instead of trying to fight with the incomers - why not help them, welcome them in fact, provide easy access for them - do everything they ask - provide a plank across the stream - so to speak. Don't put obstacles in their path - but clear the road for them - greet them as liberators.

'Of course you can imagine the reaction of the tribesmen - they were shocked that a Welsh man should suggest such a thing - until he explained the true object of the exercise, then they praised him and claimed the idea as their own. Some ignorant old diehards could not understand the purpose of it and nicknamed him Ogmore the Cringe - most unfairly in my opinion - that's why I have named his system Ogmore's Plank - to redress the insult done to Ogmore - who was most cruelly butchered by his own people as a coward, once they fully understood his method of beating the enemy - typical of the Tafia even now come to think of it...

'Poor Ogmore, he died unrecognised as the one true saviour of Welsh Culture - but his secret was too valuable to be broadcast so he had to die. The Chieftains of the time kept the secret among a handful of chosen men who wielded it with great effect against the Romans, the English, the French - anyone who came to Wales in fact. They passed on the code of practise down through the ages.

'The Society became more and more hidden as the members refined Ogmore's original concept - now only the very few top members - the Tadgis - the Grandfathers as they are known - know the membership. The rituals are a dark, severely guarded secret - I don't know them - but I have heard rumours...' He became pensive for a while... 'Yes, yes...'

'Forgive me sir' said Rupert - afraid that the Professor was not going to tell him any more... 'Forgive me' he repeated 'but I am not quite clear as to just how they operate - I mean today...'

'Today' shouted the Professor making Rupert jump - 'Yes today boy...but now they are evil - power-lusting men. They will stop at nothing to gain their end, and they are everywhere - big business - little business - sport - education - the arts - anywhere where power and English money is to be found! How do they operate?'

He leaned forward over Rupert 'They administrate - administrate boy - at every level they administrate - it's perfect... the plank you see? Never say 'no'! You can't argue with 'yes' can you?' Suddenly he was staring at Rupert with unseeing eyes, his voice trailed off - he coughed, then choked and fell across Rupert so that they both fell to the floor...

Rupert struggled from underneath the Professor and knelt beside him - loosening his collar, not quite knowing what else he should do - when the door opened and a young woman came in. She was severely dressed in a grey serge suit - her hair was tied back in a tight bun, she carried a folder. She looked at the Professor on the floor and then at Rupert, then she dropped the folder and screamed and made for the door, but before she could reach it, the Professor spoke from the floor -

'It's all right Glynis, I'm all right - no need to scream - just one of my attacks...'

He struggled to his feet and clutched at Rupert -

'I am sorry young man, but I do get over-excited sometimes and that's bad for me - I really must learn to control myself - but this has been my life's work - you understand. Oh by the way - this is my secretary - Glynis - don't know what I would do without her...'

Glynis was still staring at Rupert - white faced - the Professor stared at her -

'What's the matter with you - girl? You've seen me like that many times - you have never screamed before...' Glynis dragged her eyes away from Rupert and smiled wanly at the Professor -

'Oh I am sorry Professor, I just don't know what came over me... it was seeing this gentleman standing over you broke a dream of mine - see?' She picked up the file - walked to the desk and put the file down - turning to Rupert -

'Oh do forgive me Mr Er...?'

'Williams' said Rupert quickly... 'er Vivian Williams...'

She stared at him...'Vivian? It's a nice name...' She smiled and Rupert saw that although she was plainly dressed she was in fact very attractive.... The professor moved round to the desk -

'Glynis - do you think you could find us some tea - I do feel a bit shaky.'

'Of course Professor' - she turned to go, giving Rupert another smile.

The Professor went to the desk and sat down - he picked up his pipe and - taking a small pen knife from his pocket - he carefully cleaned the pipe - then filled it from a pouch that he produced from his pocket - he looked up at Rupert, then slowly he spoke - 'Mr Williams, I know you must be thinking that you are in the company of a mad man, but please bear with me - this thing is bigger than either of us... But I am an old man and no-one will listen to me...' He seemed about to cry - he held up his hand in a gesture of defence as Rupert tried to say something 'No - don't try to tell me otherwise - I know - I have studied this thing for so long now I am used to the way that people react to my suggestions. Mr Williams, I tell you that these people - the Tafia - are fiendish, they make the Chinese seem simple minded peasants...' Rupert was trying to understand all that was happening, but he could not see how the so-called Tafia operated - or what it had to do with his present assignment -

'I am most grateful to you sir for your time and the information.'

'But what has it to do with your problem eh?' the Professor jumped in -

'Well yes' - said Rupert -

'Much more than you think... you see it has all to do with winning... being number one... getting there first... yes, yes...' He paused and very carefully lit his pipe - smoke billowed up and he concentrated on tasting the tobacco - then a smile lit up his face - 'I didn't think she had found this lot.' Rupert looked puzzled, then remembered the wife and the weeds....

'Yes, yes' - repeated the Professor - 'let me put it simply to you Mr Williams - what is most important - winning or being the winner?'

At the risk of seeming stupid Rupert answered - 'Well sir - I rather thought that it was the same thing.'

'Ah, well there you are quite wrong Mr Williams - now we are getting somewhere -'

Rupert thought that they were getting nearer to complete madness but said nothing -

'Yes, now we are getting to the absolute nub of the matter' the Professor puffed away at the pipe happily. 'You see, Mr Williams - despite your name, you are English - you think like an Englishman, you behave like an Englishman - and of course like all true Englishmen you imagine all people are much the same as you - if maybe a little inferior - no no - don't protest - it is true...'

Rupert wanted to protest, but he knew that the Professor was right...

'Now the Welshman is different... whether the English like it or not! Now to an Englishman - it's play up, play up and play the game... it matters not the winning - the game's the thing - what ho, tally ho and all that. But when you think about it - that is silly - what matters is who has the power - who wins!'

He stopped to take a long puff at the now well-lit pipe…

'And it is this fact that the Tafia latched onto hundreds of years ago. But they could not defeat their enemies in open combat, so they let the invaders think that they were in command - do you see - they mastered the art of the figure head - whilst all the time they were really controlling everything from the administrative level - the plank over the stream - it is so simple. Let the princes come and walk about like lords of all creation - the real power when it comes to the crunch is with the little man who controls the draw-bridge - isn't it?'

The Professor sat back in his chair and Rupert saw that his eyes were closing - the pipe dropped out of his hand onto the desk, still burning well. Rupert leapt up to stop the pipe from falling to the ground as the door opened and in walked the secretary with a tray of tea -

'Ah - he's fallen asleep – well, well - you must have tired him out Mr... er... Williams - yes - he usually has a sleep this time of day. You will have to leave now' - she continued - 'I hope you have all the information you wanted?'

Rupert stood holding the pipe, and feeling rather foolish he handed the pipe to the girl - 'Ah yes thank you... yes... it is all very interesting - well, I will get along!' He walked towards the door - the girl took no notice of him but was busy making the Professor more comfortable - Rupert went out.

Once he was in the street - he started to think over all that he had learned - that took him about one minute and so feeling very depressed he made his way back to the hotel. The Chief of D.I.E. had sent him to see the Professor in the hope that he might pick up some useful information - Rupert was sure that the Professor was a brilliant man but like a lot of brilliant men, no one of a lesser greatness could make head or tail of him...

At least Rupert was now staying at a decent hotel back in Cardiff and using his new name and identity. His room was light, airy and modern and had its own bathroom - this was more like being a real agent. As he entered the lobby he began to feel a bit happier - he went to the desk for his key and was handed an envelope addressed to him as V. Williams. Wondering what it could be - he went up in the lift to his room. He did not notice the small dwarf-like man standing in one of the telephone booths near to the reception desk - which was just as well under the circumstances. In his room he opened the envelope, inside was a theatre ticket and a cryptic note: *Tonight 7.30 You are expected - D.I.E.* The D.I.E. told him it was from his Boss - but who was expecting him? He decided to take a shower and marshal his thoughts.

8   Arts and Grafts

Rupert eased his aching limbs for the thousandth time, shivered with sudden movement and cursed all obscure, brilliant Professors.... If only that daft old goat at the university had been able to spell it out in simple lay terms, all the problems would now have been solved, Rupert would have been back in glorious Putney, his mother and father would be happy parents again - instead it looked as though the story of his death was going to be made all too true. For now he knew the whole truth and they were not going to let him tell anyone - let alone his own Department.

He remembered the night at the Theatre - when it had started to become a bit clearer. He had been excited that evening, all in all, life was good, he was as near to being a real agent as he would ever be, he was going to the Theatre but at the same time he was doing his undercover job. The only thing missing was the beautiful girl called Whisper, or Honey or Deirdre! He stopped daydreaming and dressed for the evening... Dark grey slacks, brown slip on shoes, a pale blue denim shirt, leather tie and brushed pigskin jacket. He looked in the mirror and hated the image that was projected back to him - but he suffered it. After all it was a disguise only and tonight he was going to the Theatre - under cover - as someone who was vaguely connected with the British Arts Council, and tonight he was to meet some of the top dignitaries of the Welsh Arts... This had all been arranged by the Chief who had told him that information had been received that Blanchard the dead agent had been working on something to do with theatre fraud or plot stealing - however, no-one was quite sure how far he had penetrated before his death - so it had been decided to send Rupert in to scout around and just test the atmosphere. It was hoped that nobody would connect him in any way with Blanchard - in any way at all - thought Rupert - despite his new image.

One last look in the mirror - a quick flick with the comb through the now black hair with the wayward quiff that had a habit of falling over his forehead - and he was ready. He had called a cab - as he was not sure where the Theatre was situated. He had dined on a light meal of scampi and French fries followed by a half bottle of a pert burgundy. As there was to be a reception at the Theatre, it being a first night of a new play - he made a vow to himself not to drink too much, he wanted to keep his wits about him and watch for any clues that may lead him to the solution of the problems of Blanchard and the mysterious Tafia...

Not being used to provincial Theatre, Rupert became somewhat alarmed when the cab drove away from the main well-lit streets of Cardiff and started to weave its way through what seemed to be a very run down and seedy area of the City - 'Are you sure we are going to the right place?' he asked the driver -

'Yes' - the driver grunted, Rupert noticed that they were passing under a black grimed railway bridge...

'I noticed a Theatre back in the main centre' said Rupert - who had noticed that they had passed a brightly lit theatre that looked most inviting - in fact his spirits had risen as they approached it and now were sinking fast -

'Ah - that was the real Theatre' said the driver, without any apparent humour 'The one you want is down here by the railway tracks - it's the posh one - the arty grafty one!'

The street they were now in seemed dark and lined with tall dark foreboding Victorian houses, it didn't remind Rupert much of Shaftesbury Avenue or the Charing Cross

Road... And as for the 'arty crafty' he was sure that was what the driver had meant - oh god - he thought - was he in for a cultural evening? The cab stopped outside what seemed to be a huge blank prison wall - with two dimly lit glass doors at its base. 'Is this it?' Rupert did not like the look of it much - where were the coloured lights - the photos - the people?

'This is it... wouldn't catch me in there I can tell you'

'Oh' said Rupert surprised -

'No' said the driver smiling, 'load of pansies if you ask me.'

Having seen himself in the hotel room mirror Rupert thought it wise not to comment. He just hoped that his next assignment would be as a condom tester in a girl's sixth form college. He paid the driver and approached the glass doors, they opened to reveal a large but not very welcoming foyer - the carpet was stained and the lighting was the dim yellow of old southern region railway stations at night. He went to the box office which stood to his right, a middle aged woman was painting her nails, everything was so quiet. Rupert wondered if he had come to the right place...

'Er - is there a play on here tonight?' he asked the lady. She looked at him as though he had just escaped from Broadmoor - then smiled -

'I hope so love or I could have had the night off couldn't I? You want a ticket do you?'

'No I have a ticket, I am meant to be here at 7.30!'

'Oh - you'll be for the reception then, upstairs in the art gallery love - you'll find them all up there.' She returned to her nails.

Well - thought Rupert - at least the box office ladies were up to West End standards -

He wandered up a flight of stairs and hearing the unmistakeable sound of people chattering at a party - headed for the noise. He came to some more glass doors and peering through he saw the crowd - his heart sank, they were definitely arty, but at least his clothes were well up to the mark. He entered - nobody took any notice of him but went on chattering in that inane way that people only seem to achieve at arty functions. Rupert saw that in a corner there was a table covered in wine bottles - behind which stood a bored looking girl in a long dull khaki coloured dress - her hair was straight, long and not too clean he noticed as he approached. Before he could say anything she handed him a glass and asked in a voice that matched her demeanour - 'Red or white?'

'Red - thank you' - she slopped some red wine into his glass and over his hand then turned and picked up a thick book - Rupert saw that the title was 'Feminism and the Single Lesbian' - well he didn't like girls with dirty hair anyway.

The fact that no-one took any notice of Rupert gave him the chance to study the crowd. Was the answer to his mission hidden here among these earnest arty crafty types? They stood around in small groups, talking rapidly about theatre, acting and art in general. Rupert let himself drift around the crowd, seemingly to look at the pictures arranged around the walls, presumably only there to justify calling the long narrow ordinary room the art gallery, they were certainly not here for their artistic merit, thought Rupert, who although no art expert could tell a Matisse from a mattress. These pictures were almost all the same - a few pencil lines slashed across the expensive looking paper - blots of washed out water paint apparently thrown on from a great distance and a huge, sweeping but indiscernible signature. They had names too like - Ty

Mawr at dawn - Graig a Nos at Dusk - Moonlight over the Mumbles - and so on. Rupert liked the frames though, really expensive stainless steel and glass. Nobody else in the room was taking any notice of the pictures - Rupert presumed that as this was a theatre evening, pictures were out! He overheard snatches of conversation, telling himself that he was not eves-dropping - it was his job to find out everything he could after all. In one corner a strident sounding female in a kaftan was holding forth on the subject of mime -

'Darius is all very well Nigel, but really old hat now - I mean everyone is into him aren't they? And as for Marceau - well really he is to modern mime what Agatha Christie is to serious drama my dear!'

Rupert moved on - a tall gangly man - in what seemed to be a leotard - and with bare feet - was being frank with a serious looking girl in baggy trousers and murky T Shirt.

'The whole point is, Samantha, that Jane is more suited to the part, and it was not anything personal you understand.'

'But she can't move - you know she can't move - you said so Daryl.'

'The part doesn't call for movement oriented skills, Samantha.'

'Well I hope you know what you are doing Daryl - I mean the piece is only the most significant move away from crass open ended theatre that we have seen since Myerkov!'

'I know that Samantha.'

A small thin man took Rupert's attention - he looked exactly like most people's idea of a stereotype Gestapo officer, except that he was not in uniform - the steely blue eyes darted around the room through thin gold rimmed spectacles while he spoke in clipped sentences to two totally bald young men, shaven bald, even their eyebrows.. They looked like Easter eggs on legs - thought Rupert - even the conversation was slightly sinister - the Gestapo officer was talking -

'What they don't seem to understand is that here in Cardiff we are starving - they cannot expect us to cater for them as well. This is the capital - farmers traditionally don't go to the theatre anyway…'

'You have to be ruthless Gilbert, that's all - ruthless' - this from egg one - 'Well I am - I tell them - there simply is no money to spare and that's that -'

'Quite - I mean without our new computer set up - our video scheme would fail - and we are in to forty thousand now', chipped in egg two -

Egg one: 'Your last documentary was great, Brian - just great! I mean people have shot sheep before - but not as an art subject...'

Rupert presumed that they were talking about filming - though there had been a lot of rustling in the country districts… His wanderings had brought him to another table - the buffet. One look at it and Rupert put all thought of the 'eggs' being sheep rustlers out of his mind, for here arrayed in the most tasteful way was a Vegan's delight - not even any butter or cheese - and what looked like genuine vintage, cold sliced nut cutlets - that in London had gone out with miniskirts, flower power and free love. Rupert hoped that his hotel served food late at night.

'Are you with the press?' An aggressive sharp, acid voice jarred in his left ear - he turned to see a small dark-haired girl - wearing what seemed to be the in-uniform - a long shapeless dress in a faded muddy wine colour - the hair too had the statutory uncombed and not too well washed look - she wore no makeup and an expression that almost dared Rupert to think she was ugly because of it. Rupert thought that she was very ugly - but then he was the type of male chauvinist pig who openly looked at page three girls and thought that boobs were wonderful things that should bounce with budgie type health. If this creature had any boobs they were well hidden and that was probably a good thing considering the state of her hair... Rupert had a thing about hair - 'No' -

'Well you look like press' -

'Sorry'

'You are not an actor?'

'No' -

'You are not a member of the public - are you?' This was said with the disdainful horror of Mrs Whitehouse finding a copy of Playboy in her church pew on Sunday -

'I'm from London - I have been invited to see the play tonight...' He took the ticket out of his pocket and showed it to her -

If her face had not already been the colour of uncooked pastry she would have paled - as it was she just stared at him - 'Oh my god - you're from London!'

'Yes' -

'Arts Council?'

'Seconded -'

'Oh my god - what must you think of us!'
Rupert didn't tell her -

'Carol was meant to meet you in the foyer - have you got a drink - oh my god!'

'It doesn't matter you know.'

'Of course it does, we want you to see us as we really are - you know - judge the work fairly -'

'Well yes -'

'And nobody is looking after you - Christ - just a minute I'll find Carol -'

She sped off in the direction of the foyer - leaving Rupert staring after her. He was not alone for long when another identikit female approached him -

'Have you had some food?'

'No thank you - I have eaten already' -

'Trudy will be upset - nobody is eating her food.'
The creature moved away to accost some other poor unfortunate non-eater.

Suddenly the first vinegar-voiced female was hurrying back accompanied by an important looking female, who was also wearing the standard costume - but she was additionally festooned with cheap Indianesque type bangles and beads - she had short cropped hair - the sort of style that was once the pride of the army national service barbers, only on the squaddies it looked attractive - the faint shadow of a moustache on her upper lip completed the military image. She floated up to Rupert - it was the only way he could describe her movement as her long flowing dress of pale puce and copper swept the floor as she walked, so she floated up to Rupert and gushed -

'I am so sorry - I was waiting for you but I got side tracked by a last minute hitch in the play - you know.' Rupert smiled - he wanted to run but he smiled!

'That's all right - I was just having a look around. This is a nice place.' Oh god, thought Rupert I have said it - nice place - it was a pretentious monster of a place...

'Well it has its faults, but it is functional - You are Mr Williams aren't you?'

'Oh yes - I'm from London.'

She almost simpered - and on her - it was frightening.

'I'm Carol Eaves, I am the Administrator of the Company that is performing tonight - I'm also the Director.'

'Ah!'

'Have you been to Cardiff before?'

'Before what?' asked Rupert who wasn't concentrating.

'No I mean - is this your first visit to Wales?'

'Oh yes - Yes I'm sorry - I wasn't concentrating - yes it is my first visit…'

'You will find things different from English Theatre!

'I'm sure...'

'Really?'

Rupert decided that he had better pay some attention - the conversation was taking a serious tone – 'Oh yes - we are very much into reality, through movement and mime - and the futility of words as a medium of true expression.' Rupert resisted the temptation to reply - 'Who isn't these days' or 'Quite, so confusing all these words -'

'Really', was all he said.

'Yes - this play tonight for instance is a landmark for us - yes, a landmark - do you know his work?'

'Who?'

'Rick Johnson?'

'Er… no, who is he?'

'He wrote tonight's play -'

'All - I didn't see it advertised outside...'

'No - well we don't put out posters, not outside I mean - the public might see them and want to come in - and the piece isn't ready for that yet...'

'Oh I see!'

'No - what we have here is, essentially, a performance piece of course, but with overtones of a real event, taking place in the actual time scale of... well - the real time - if you know what I mean?'

Rupert was ready to eat all the nut cutlets - this was going to be hell. 'You say you direct the company?'

'Yes, would you like a nut cutlet - only whole food you know?'

'No - I have eaten.'

'Some more wine - it's Algerian you know - we won't have South African stuff here -'

'Oh no - quite.'

'Except the grapefruit' -

'Yes'

'I am also the Administrator of the Company'

'Does that mean you get two salaries?' joked Rupert

The look on her face told Rupert that she was not amused! 'What department did you say you were from Mr Williams?'

'Assessment - group seven - mainly observation you know.'

'Then you don't know a great deal about the set-up here in Wales?'

'No - the idea is to see for ourselves what is happening in the regions - it was thought better to send someone who was not too familiar with the area they are covering - you see?' Rupert sincerely hoped she did because he didn't.

'Ah yes I understand perfectly and it makes sense of course... well I will try and explain everything to you as far as I can'

'Thank you! '

'Are you sure you won't have some food?' The acid voiced one had crept up on them.

'No really - I had some food at my hotel - honest' - he smiled his best chat-up-the-birds smile - it failed.

'Oh well we'll have some for tomorrow's cafe buffet'

She retreated to the back of the room and talked earnestly to the girl on the wine table -

'The point is...' the Boss Woman was talking again - Rupert tried to pay full attention - 'The thing is that there is no real comparison with English and Welsh culture - what we are trying to do is find a middle road'

'Oh I see - and this Company - is it all Welsh then?' She stared at him aghast -

'God - no - that would be a bit obvious wouldn't it?'

'Oh yes - yes of course... what I meant was that I have never heard of this Company or this Theatre...' She took his arm and led him slightly away from the main crowd - which seemed to be growing bigger and noisier. 'This Company can in all reality be likened to the National Theatre in London!'

Rupert's spirits started an upward climb - he was a real fan of the National Theatre in London - it was a great place to meet people - the bars were good and you could always impress girls if you had a couple of tickets for the latest Peter Hall production or Roman Extravaganza - yes this sounded more like it -

'Well, I must say that sounds great' - he said - 'I suppose then you have had your top actors all working together for years. Who are your top actors by the way?' The lady was giving him a decidedly odd look - 'I'm sorry - have I said something wrong - you must forgive me - but as you said - I am bound to find some differences - what I meant - well you said - that is - well now - how long has the Company been together then? I mean it's just that I haven't heard of them, you see - I have heard of the National Theatre and Sheffield Theatre Crucible - and

Nottingham Playhouse... and the Abbey Dublin and the Glasgow Citizens Theatre - and all those - you know - but somehow I seemed to have missed this one - what is it called by the way?'

The lady was now glaring at him –

'Mr Williams - I realise that it is a deliberate ploy to send down someone who does not know anything about Welsh Culture and Theatre - and I do of course see the sense of it - but to make a comparison between what we are doing here and the Rep companies you mentioned is crass - honestly! I mean this Company is the Premier Company of Wales, Mr Williams, and this is the Number One Theatre Venue!' The way she used the word 'Rep' was to describe a pickled onion floating in your cup of tea; Rupert realised that he was not making a very good impression on the lady Director.

'I am so sorry - I did not mean to denigrate your work in any way - I was just puzzled that I had not come across it before…'

She looked at him a little more kindly. 'Ah yes, and I am sorry too - we Welsh you know are a little sensitive about our Heritage.'

'Sorry - you are Welsh then?' Rupert asked as she sounded Sloane with undertones of Lewisham -

'By adoption! Now about this Company - you have to understand that there might be a few problems tonight as this is the first time they have worked together.'

'I see' said Rupert, who didn't at all.

'This is the new National Theatre of Wales! It's not called that yet, but that's what it is in essence - yes!'

'When was the Company formed then?'

'Well two months ago actually, it is the most exciting thing to happen to Welsh Theatre in years - I can tell you...'

'Er... so there hasn't been any main theatre activity here in Wales then - until now I mean?'

She looked stunned. 'Of course there has Mr Williams - there is a great tradition of Theatre stretching back to the nineteen sixties in Cardiff alone - only before it was sporadic - no central company and you will agree - I hope - that a Country like Wales should have a National Theatre??'

'Oh yes - well I mean - of course!'

Rupert drank some of the Algerian wine and thought that something about this evening was reminiscent of Alice in Wonderland.... The Company he was about to see had never worked together before, in fact the Company had only just been formed, and yet it was the Number One Company in the Country! There was no doubt about it - Welsh Theatre was very different to its English counterpart. He wondered what the play would be like...

'The play you are going to see is absolutely brilliant!' said the Director - 'The Press are over-board about it, you know, he must be our most exciting writer!'

'But I thought you said that the play hasn't been performed yet?' Rupert knew as he said this that it would elicit a rebuff type logical answer - but he had to ask.

'No of course it hasn't - tonight is the world premiere - but the Press know all about the play and the writer and as this is the Premier Company - well naturally it would not be performing any rubbish would it? Therefore they know that the play is a success!'

Well he had known it would be something like that - he was getting the hang of the game now - he felt quite excited - he could go back to London as an expert on this strange ethnic theatre.

A bell sounded - the play was about to begin. The Lady Director led Rupert towards two double doors that looked as though they led to the Theatre, 'I will introduce you to the other people later on.' She smiled and simpered again...

Oh dear, thought Rupert, she was going to sit next to him for sure. They entered a dark auditorium, Rupert could see that the stage was set - the curtains were not in use tonight. On stage was what looked like a cut-away version of a broken down coffee bar... He was guided to his seat as the final house lights dimmed. 'What is the play called? he hastily asked the Lady Director -

'Gethin's Last Stand, revisited' - she sat back contented. The play began. The memory of that night was to stay with Rupert for the rest of his life as one of the most remarkable and incredible theatre experiences.

The play opened normally enough, with a woman wandering onto the set and sitting at a stool near the bar of the cafe. She sat for a long time, then slowly lit a cigarette... coughed long and hard then she spoke with a high nasal Welsh accent that is only ever heard in such plays - in such theatres - spoken by English actors -

'Fuck!... Fuck!... Fuck!... (COUGH, COUGH) Fuck!'... There was a long pause, then a small dark limping man entered carrying a tray of dirty cups, he looks at the woman for a long time then walked to the counter then spoke:

'You'll have to give it up you know...'

'Piss off cripple, where's Carlos?'

'Piss off yourself, whore, how would I know - Carlos is a law unto himself - as you well know!'... The woman then threw herself into a chair and wept, and cried:

'Why does he do this to me... He knows I love him don't he?'

'He'll never be true to you, you fool - things have changed...'

Rupert's head reeled for the next hour and a half, as the plot unfolded - it turned out that the cafe was at the end of the docks and had been a well-known and prosperous place in its heyday - but now that the big ships had gone, it was run down and derelict - mainly due - as far as Rupert could work out, to the English Government having refused a Home Rule Law for Wales. The first act ended with the sudden arrival of Carlos - a tall sinister character, who for some reason had a guttural German accent - there was a black-out as he spoke one word - 'Christ!' - a few hands clapped - whether in appreciation or because the heating was not working - Rupert was not sure - Carol, the Director, grabbed Rupert's hand and led him out to the foyer which was now full of people crushed around the bar. This surprised Rupert as he was sure there hadn't been that many in the Theatre.

'Cretins!' muttered the Lady Director - 'they are only here to see the James Bond crap in the other auditorium.'

Rupert longed to join them. A glass of wine was thrust into his hands, and he seemed to be surrounded by earnest types - all chattering away.

'Isn't it great... such realism... that opening - I mean so... right? Yes - wonderful scope... and depth of feeling... His symbolism is so strong... I mean one can see the whole connection... so black and white...' Rupert looked longingly at the front doors, but he knew he would have to stay as he had learned nothing yet that affected his mission...

'You don't look very impressed...' - this came from a tall - balding and slightly overweight man in his middle forties and wearing tinted blue glasses... he was clutching a pint glass in which Rupert saw enviously was lager.

'If you tell me where you got the lager - I will tell you what I think of the play' he said -

'It's a deal' laughed the new man... 'You get it at the bar just like in a real pub, but if you are arty - you don't have a pint - very common.' He spoke with a well-modulated Home Counties accent with overtones of BBC radio announcers...

'I am not really arty - I'll have a pint!'

'Oh - I thought you were the tame Arts Council man they are all so worried about' - he pulled out a packet of king-size cigarettes - offered one to Rupert, deftly took one himself with his teeth - put the packet away pulled out a Zippo - performed one of the more flashy tricks of lighting it and leaned across a group of smaller people - 'Tom - give us two more lagers will you?'

Rupert was impressed - he had been trying to master that trick with a Zippo for months - 'I'm impressed' he said laughing, this was the first real person he had met.

'Silly really isn't it?' as he spoke he leaned over again and handed Rupert a pint of lager 'Cheers - now your part of the bargain?'

Rupert took a long drink from his lager, sighed, then looked at the man who had provided it...

'Do you want my honest opinion?' He somehow felt that this man was not of the same breed as the airy fairy ones around the foyer…

'Please yourself - the truth would - I think - be more fun though'.

'Well to be perfectly truthful, I haven't a clue what is going on...' He looked around to make sure no-one else was paying him any attention then - 'I mean - to be honest it just seems like a bad night in a Pinter cafe, only Pinter didn't write the dialogue...' The tall man laughed, finished his pint, leaned over towards the bar and grabbed another -

'I like it - yes I think you have got it - but don't tell this lot - they think it's the second coming of Shakespeare - but then no-one has told them about Theatre beyond Offa's Dyke - it would be too cruel!' Rupert found himself laughing now -

'Forgive me, but you don't sound as though you belong among this lot yourself... so what...?' He left the question in the air...

'What am I doing here? Ah well you see I run a theatre - oh don't look worried - I mean a real one that has to rely on people coming to see the shows, for money - I work up in the hills near Brecon...' At the mention of Brecon, Rupert looked sharply at the stranger but he looked friendly enough.... 'I come down here now and again to harass the Arts Council and this lot of phonies - it's fun - trouble is they have all the money - all the administrators do - it's a bloody Tafia!' Rupert nearly dropped his lager.

'What did you say?'

'It's a joke, you know like the Mafia, only centred around the River Taff - Tafia!' He finished his lager, took Rupert's now empty glass, 'We have time for another before the onslaught of Act Two.'

He leaned over again and shouted for more lager.... 'Are you doing anything after the show - I should like to talk to you about the set up here - in more detail' asked Rupert. He thought that this man might be an ally, anyway he did seem to know the theatre set-up and that could be useful...

'Oh - I'm free, if you can get away from the culture ghouls - we'll go to a bar I know - coldest lager in Wales...' The bell sounded - 'Here we go - wouldn't you rather join this lot and see Bond beating the hell out of the Russians?' He laughed.

'I would but I am working.'

'This isn't work friend; this is slavish dedication beyond the call of duty...' Suddenly the Lady Director appeared at Rupert's side looking flushed and worried...

'Oh there you are - I am so sorry - I lost sight of you... oh my god what are *you* doing here?' This last was directed at the stranger.

'Hello Carol, I see you haven't improved your style of direction - that two day seminar at Monmouth Castle didn't help then, pity!' He was smiling but Rupert could see that underneath he was quite angry. The lady just glared at him then turned to Rupert...

'We have to be getting back Mr Williams as the second half is starting...' She dragged at Rupert's elbow almost desperately.... He followed her - looking forward to later in the evening, but realising that he had not asked the stranger's name. The second half of the play was a riot in Rupert's mind as he watched it with the knowledge that there was somewhere in the audience a fellow non-believer. Even to Rupert's untrained eye some of the dialogue and acting was excruciating.... with the lady with the cough still protesting her love for Carlos - who turned out despite his German accent to be a local Welsh lad, the product of a German sailor and a lady of ill repute called Gladys.

He had gone to the bad and become a pimp - and in the good old days had run a string of girls from the coffee bar at the end of the bay - which was owned by Gethin the cripple - who had not always been a cripple but had been injured by a falling bale of cotton from an English ship when he was a boy - hence his intense hatred of all things English - he was in love with the coughing lady - who had been one of Carlos's best girls but had contracted a social disease - and anyway was past it - she had caught the dose from an English sailor - so of course she hated the English.... she was also in love with Carlos but he despised her and spent his time bemoaning the fact that the English had taken the ships away and his trade - he also hated the English on account of his being half German.

Various smaller characters wandered on and off, all hating the English and reminiscing about the old days when Gethin's bar was all action. After another hour and a bit the play came to a conclusion with a sickening thud as Carlos - for some reason Rupert could not quite understand, stabbed the cripple to death with a steak knife, whilst screaming that it was all his fault and calling him father... at the same time the cough lady screamed and rolled about the floor in simulated sex, screaming that it was not the little cripple's fault... The final scene ended when the door burst open and there stood a tall man in a torn raincoat. He was soaking wet - although up to that point there had been no indication of rain - Carlos stopped stabbing the cripple - the woman stopped writhing - they both stared at the newcomer then with a scream the woman shouted 'Gethin - you stupid fucking bastard...' and there was a merciful blackout.

In the silence that followed Rupert made his way to the foyer, hoping he could dash away quickly with the stranger and get very pissed on cold lager.... If Blanchard - whose death he was investigating - had had to suffer this - then suicide would seem logical - leeks, rugby ball an all! Rupert never made it to the door - the long dressed brigade led by the Lady Director descended upon him and led him upstairs once more to the Art Gallery where more wine and whole food was waiting for the celebration that was to follow this most stimulating of evenings... Rupert noticed with relief that the stranger was there too - magically it seemed to Rupert - clutching another pint of lager. He seemed to be talking to a serious looking middle aged man in a corner.

Rupert was borne off to meet the author, the cast and the top people from the Local Arts Council. The Lady Director, having shoved a glass of red in his hand and said for him to meet Rick Johnson - the writer... who to Rupert's surprise seemed to be a normal person... until he spoke -

'I suppose you hated it - didn't you' he accused Rupert and dared him to deny it -

'Don't be so paranoid Ricky...' the Director saved Rupert from answering, 'it was just great! I have just seen the crit., super! The audience on the whole though was moribund... but we expect that don't we?' she laughed...

'God - if the public liked my work - I would give up and buy a farm' - this strange remark came from the author, who Rupert realised was rather drunk....

 'No chance of that Ricky dear' quipped a precious looking male dressed in pink, and who Rupert just recognised as Gethin from the play...'no chance... god the public are thick - don't you think so?' He looked straight at Rupert

'Oh - well now... you see... I'm not... that is...'

'God!' This seemed to be the pink man's favourite word. 'God - you are the Arts Council man?'

'Yes' said Rupert - glad to be on comparatively safe ground -

'Oh well, I suppose you have to be a bit cagey, I, as an artist, I couldn't stand your job - god - I must be free to express myself... you know!'

'We all bloody know Freda' - mumbled the author...

The man in pink, just stared at the author, then shrugged - the Director was talking to Rupert now, 'Don't take any notice of them, Mr Williams... listen, may I call you by your Christian name?'

'Yes - why not' said Rupert -

'What is it?' sweetly from the Director -

'What?' said Rupert... 'Oh sorry - yes it's Ru...Vivian'... he shuddered inwardly, as the man in pink sniggered and simpered at the same time - not a pretty sight

'Well Vivian, as I said - don't take any notice of them - they are just excited - letting off steam - it takes it out of you - you know - creative work!' He didn't know what it did for them but Rupert felt exhausted...

'Oh I am sure - yes - well it was a most unusual evening...'

'Unusual!' slurred the author... 'In what way unusual eh?'

'Well, it is my first experience of Welsh Theatre you know?'

'Ha - you call this Welsh Theatre do you?' Rupert could see that the author was in fact very drunk...

'Fuck Welsh Theatre - just keep the bloody English money coming, sunshine!' He was grabbed from behind and hauled away by one of the very bald men Rupert had seen earlier...

'Sorry about that Vivian' - the Lady Director - 'he was very much influenced by Dylan Thomas you know...'

'Was he? I like Dylan's work...'

'Very passé now, though, don't you think... I see Ricky going on where Thomas stopped you know...' Rupert could see that Ricky had made it to the drinks table and was tilting a bottle to his lips... he could see what the Director meant, and thought it a pity that the author had not been influenced by Dylan's writing...

'Where are you staying Vivian?' The Director was looking at him with a strange hard look, and he hated the way that she had said the name Vivian.

'Oh - at the Harp Hotel - you know...' He had no idea why he lied to her... perhaps it was some sixth sense he had developed since being an agent. Or more likely - he thought - just a kind of terror of having her turn up outside his bedroom in the early hours of the morning... he shuddered.

'Oh!' she stared at him for a moment - then added... 'Well, if you are in town for a few days, you must come up to my office for a coffee and a chat and things... be less crowded there...' She stared across the room to where the Brecon Theatre man was standing - there was an ugly look on her face - as well as a couple of spots - Rupert really hated spots!

'Yes of course' he answered remembering his cover story... 'Yes I would like that...'

'What would you like?' The Director had turned back to him and was staring at him with doe like eyes - or was it dough like - he wondered...

'Oh - you know... er coffee and that...'

'Oh yes and that...' Rupert felt panic... she was drunk, whether from booze or power he didn't know - but the effect was the same... she gripped his arm and he realised that she was very strong... she was probably one of these women who went in for body building! He felt trapped and looked around in desperation for his one ally! There was no sight of the Brecon Man... He turned back to the Director - God - he thought - even his hero - Bond - had never had to face such a hideous adversary... at least his women - however evil - were feminine. He was about to try and pull away from the vice like grip when a hand landed on his shoulder and a friendly voice spoke...

'Come on - old mate - you and I have a date with a gallon or two of real lager.'

The grip on his arm was immediately released and he turned gratefully to face the Brecon Man. As he did so, he could see the look in the Director's face - the red rimmed eyes were blazing with barely controlled hate… She lasered the Brecon man and hissed...

'Why don't you piss off - you money grubbing philistine...' Rupert noticed that her slight Sloane accent had gone and in its place was pure Saturday-Night Lewisham... The Brecon man just laughed and said -

'Ah Carol my dear - you are so attractive when you are just being yourself... so much prettier too. Bye now - sorry I can't stay for the real party - but us common commercial theatre types have to keep in touch with the real people - night!'

He turned Rupert round and led him towards the doors. Rupert turned to get one last glimpse of the Lady Director striding purposefully in the direction of the two bald pansies, as he was whisked out into the night - in the company of a total stranger.

9   Reflections in Iced Cold Lager

Rupert was convinced that - for the first time in history - dawn was going to fail to arrive. He shifted his legs for the thousandth time that night, but it didn't help, whatever position he adopted was sheer agony. Bond would have registered the pain, put it to the back of his mind, thought of the girl in question and fought on.

Rupert only wanted to cry - why oh why he asked himself over and over again, why hadn't he seen the warning signs in time and why, even when he had spotted the clues, hadn't he just reported them to his boss and got the hell out of the firing line? Oh no - he had to follow his hero's example and try to see it through alone.

He remembered how the Brecon theatre man had bundled him into a battered old car and driven him at speed through the backstreets and into the centre of Cardiff where he had parked outside a large and expensive looking Hotel. He led Rupert down to a cellar bar which was darkly lit and friendly, purchased two tankards of lager and kept silent as they sat on bar stools and drank. The Brecon man finished his pint almost in one gulp, indicated to the barman, who was obviously used to the routine, came and refilled the glass, only then did the Brecon man speak.

'Christ - but that's better. I have to get the taste of that place out of my mouth'. He sank a good half of his new pint - 'You are probably wondering why I go there if I hate it so much eh?'

'Er - well – yes!' Rupert had indeed been wondering...

'Well you see - Viv old lad - it's simple really - I run a small theatre way up in the hills and sometimes I wonder whether the work I am doing is any good - so I pop down to see what is happening in the great theatres of our noble country - and I go back feeling sick but strangely confident that I am on the right course.' Rupert watched in wonder as he finished the rest of his pint and nodded for another...

'Are they always that bad then?' he asked. The Brecon man looked at him and smiled -

'Good god no' - he laughed at some inner secret... 'No - sometimes they have a go at the great writers - non-Welsh writers - Shakespeare even - and then I really start drinking - but I will say at least they are funny - you know on the basis that they are so bad that they are almost good theatre...' He drank deep again.

'I am a bit puzzled by something that the Director told me' said Rupert finishing his first pint and seeing its replacement appear as though by magic. 'What's that?'

'Well - how can it be the major theatre company in Wales when this is their first production and the cast have never worked together before?' The Brecon man smiled benignly at him...

'Ah - I can see you need the standard lecture on Welsh Theatre old lad' - he leaned across the bar and had two full pints lined up with the others on the counter - 'so we won't be disturbed' he explained - then he gave Rupert a cigarette and lit one himself, settled back comfortably on his stool and started... 'You - like me - are used to thinking about theatre as it is in England and particularly London - where there is great competition and where - with a few minor exceptions - the best work tends to get on and do well - right?'

Rupert nodded...

'Well now - in Wales things are very different in many ways - first and most important there are very few theatres or theatre companies here, and what there are, are almost all controlled by the Arts Council - there is no independent commercial theatre - apart from the odd summer seasons at the seaside towns and there are not that many of those...' He paused as though collecting his thoughts... 'So what you have here is really one theatre made up of a handful of companies all controlled by a central body the Arts Council and its acolytes the Regional Arts Associations - between them they dictate what shall and shall not be done. Now, couple this power with a desire to be big fish in a puddle and a tendency to ignore anything that goes on the other side of Offa's Dyke and you start to get the picture. The outcome is you have a kind of artistic mafia or' - he smiled - 'as I said earlier - Tafia!'

Rupert nearly choked on his pint, coughed and felt cold all over. 'You all right - old chap?' The Brecon man was studying him closely...

'Oh yes', lied Rupert, 'just not used to this lager you know?'

'Oh right!' The Brecon man looked oddly at Rupert... 'Right - well to continue - this little group of people guard their right to dictate theatre policy very jealously and they make very sure that nobody from outside comes in and starts rocking the boat...' He took a long drink then continued. 'As with all things of course - there is a lot of money involved and that is what they protect most - the actual standard of work doesn't really matter as long as the gang all remain in the loop...'

'Something else that has been puzzling me' said Rupert in the brief pause -

'What?'

'Why are so few of the people I met tonight Welsh?'

'Ah ah...' the Brecon man beamed...' Now you have it Viv...'

'I have?'

'Yes' - he sighed - 'It has always been the same you know - all great patriots throughout history have either been late converts or complete outsiders in love with a dream - Hitler - Napoleon - Byron - the list is endless... it is slightly different here - the pushers here are not so much fanatics in love with the country as English failures and half-Welsh dropouts who have found the arts a good soft option. For instance you will find that so called Welsh theatre is dripping with failed or inadequate teachers...' - he stopped - blinked his eyes a few times - 'Sorry, must be the lights in here - too bright - where was I - oh yes - well to your question - as I said only a handful of people benefit from the arts money given to Wales and they want to keep it that way - so what they do - to make it look as though there is a lot going on - is to keep changing the main companies and claiming that each one is a new and greater innovation in the land - whereas in fact it is the same old group just throwing up a smokescreen... and they have to keep changing the cast because if an actor who wasn't part of the club stayed for long - he would soon see how phony the set up was...

'It's a neat system really - the only people who make any kind of a living from the arts grants are the administrators - all the artists are on minimum pay and contracts - even the writers. They have a wonderful group here you know - they pick a playwright of sorts and do rehearsed readings of his or her play - sometimes even a production - they call it a competition - so that although they, the administrators, get the full pay - the writers get the prize - a few bob - and the thrill, ha! - of seeing their play mutilated out of all recognition by a director... like the one you saw tonight - but it keeps the real money in the family whilst making it look as though so much is being done for new writers... Now you take that back to your masters in London, Rupert old chap...'

So saying he slumped forward slowly onto the bar and after mumbling a few phrases like 'beware the administrators' and 'they couldn't direct traffic' - he fell asleep.... Rupert was at a loss for a moment and puzzled. If what this man had said was true then much was wrong here. Why had he kept mentioning the Tafia... and did he know something about Rupert's mission - had he been planted on him? It was all very confusing and the Algerian wine followed by the lager did not help his thinking process.

The barman came over - saw the Brecon man - then told Rupert that he would be out for hours but that as he was a resident it didn't matter. Rupert then ordered a cab to take him to his hotel - his head felt very thick and he could not think very clearly but as he was being driven along it cleared very suddenly and he became very cold indeed - as he remembered that just before he had fallen asleep the strange theatre man from Brecon had called him Rupert

10   Some Men of Harlech

There was something crawling up Rupert's leg - panic was creeping up his mind - what lived in old oak trees in Wales? As far as he could think there were no tarantulas, scorpions or black cobras - no asps - rattle snakes or tree climbing alligators resident in the Principality - but something was moving up his leg towards his kneecap - inside his trousers. He thought with longing about his hotel room in Cardiff - how sweet now the thought of a plate of laver bread - even raw seaweed would be something he thought, as his stomach rumbled again - it seemed like a month since he had eaten.... was it only three days since he came up here to Harlech.... Harlech! How often he had heard that song 'Men of Harlech' - he never really thought about it being a place somehow... He thought about it like the song 'Hearts of Oak' - 'Men of Harlech'. Ah well - he thought again for the hundredth time in that long vigil of the last big mistake he had made in Cardiff - how simple and gullible he had been.... how stupid... how blind...

He had gone straight to his room on returning from his experience with the man from Brecon - and on entering he checked the hairs he had carefully placed across the door - then saw on the mat on the floor - an envelope; he had picked it up and opened it and read the letter inside - which considering his consumption that evening was no mean feat - he thought. The letter read:

'Dear Vivian, I hope that your visit to our Theatre tonight was a pleasant experience for you and that you arrived home safely. This is just a note to let you know that there is a meeting of the full Drama Panel in two days time up in Harlech - and we were wondering if you had the time to come up and join us. I am sure you would find

the trip exciting and interesting and I know that any queries you might have could all be answered. Do please try and come, the meeting starts at two in the local Theatre building but if you could manage to arrive by one o'clock I could introduce you to the important people. Regards etc. P.S. Do be careful when dealing with that person from Brecon - all is not what it seems!'

It was written in the voice of and signed by - Carol Eaves, Director, Administrator and Arts Council Panellist - at the bottom was the address of the Hotel in Harlech. He read it several times before the full import of it hit him. Then he read it again - to make sure he had understood it properly. Afterwards he was to regret that he had not got in touch with his Boss in London and handed it all to them, but at the time it all seemed very exciting and Bondish. Later, much later - he remembered that he had told the Director that he was staying at the Harp Hotel - by then though it was too late - much too late.

The following morning he made two crucial mistakes - the first was in ordering laver bread with his standard English breakfast - the second equally serious - in its way - was in deciding to drive up to Harlech the day before the meeting was due to take place. He thought it would give him the chance to relax and get his bearings - relax! Both these errors had uncomfortable and painful repercussions - the first almost before he could reach his bedroom and blessed private loo - the second several days later.

But for the moment he was happy enough - somehow he thought that he was getting closer to the truth behind poor Blanchard's death - and once he had done that he could get back to Putney and sanity. Therefore, early the following morning he booked out of his comfortable Hotel, having spent most of the previous day between trying to contact the local representative of D.I.E. and failing - and sitting in his Hotel bathroom and succeeding.

He drove to the Wharf where the local office was situated but could still get no response - so he left a note under the door and headed north in the small hired Ford Fiesta - courtesy of The Firm. Maintaining his now legendary skill as a navigator - he broke his journey north in the small market town of Llandovery - where he had a splendid lunch and a drink in Ye Old Kings Head Inn - and a chat with the jovial landlord - who it turned out was something of a poet and was currently working on a series of short poems describing his customers... Rupert left before he too was put in the book - agents had to remain anonymous after all. He arrived in the quaint castle town of Harlech late in the afternoon and set out at once to find accommodation.

It is a proven truth that when the fates wish to really screw someone they contact the original sod of sod's law and in concert set about their chosen victim. Rupert, all unaware of the cruelty of the gods, went blithely on his way to purgatory. He found a nice out-of-the-way Hotel - which was not too expensive and looked clean and when he approached the desk the receptionist even smiled - such is the low down evil cunning of the gods. Yes - they did have a single room to let with bathroom. At last - thought Rupert - things are getting better!

The room was splendid and commanded a view over a small valley to the sea. It also overlooked the front entrance of the Hotel, which proved to be its most important factor. Rupert was so pleased that he parted with a pound coin for the elderly man who had shown him to his room. When he was alone he sat on the bed and thought over the last couple of days... was he really any nearer the solution... did he in fact have any clues to help him - and why had that strange Brecon theatre man called him Rupert... that really worried him. At least he thought - for the moment he was away from it all and could have a nice relaxing evening - a good meal - a couple of drinks and watch the English programmes on T.V.

The evening started well enough. He took a shower - changed into some casual, yet trendy gear... not his own taste but suitable for someone called Vivian. He had just tested his Zippo and checked his cigarette supply and was about to go down for the first lager since the yard arm had sunk behind the sun, when he heard a car arriving at the front of the hotel. Idle curiosity caused him to walk over to the window and look out. He had read somewhere that in moments of great terror or extreme shock the hair could turn white - the blood freeze - and one's heart could stop and or leap up into one's mouth. Rupert felt as though all four had happened to him....

A large black saloon car had pulled up outside the front door - from the interior of which came - in order Iestyn Morris - Ianto Price the solicitor from Brecon - and Carol Eaves the Director.... Rupert stepped back quickly from any possible sight-line and found that although his blood was frozen he was sweating profusely... What could this mean? What was the connection between D.I.E. and the Arts Lady - and what the hell were they doing here tonight? He pulled the curtain partly across the window and using it to shield his body from sight - had another peek. Then he noticed that there was a fourth person - presumably the driver. Rupert could only see his back - then he turned to say something to Morris - Rupert shook - it was Police Inspector Evans from Cardiff.

Rupert's mind raced - what could this mean? What possible connection could there be between the arts people and the law men? He found he was sweating again - when he realised that another two minutes and he would have walked right into them at the reception desk. Before he could think anymore he heard a noise of approaching footsteps outside his door - he went over and stood with his ear up against the panel... he could hear the Director Woman talking very clearly - it seemed that they were all in rooms very close to him. He heard her saying that she was going to take a bath and that she would meet them all down in the bar in an hour. That would give him time to get a drink - thought Rupert - and he needed one. He waited until he heard the doors closing and then slipped out into the corridor and down the stairs to the bar. He ordered a pint and as casually as he could he asked the girl behind the bar if there was something special on that night.

'Oh yes' she replied 'It's a big do for the Arts Council' -

'Oh' said Rupert very disinterested...

'Yes - quite a spread too - it's a sort of party as far as I can make out - lots of guests and champagne!'

'Really?' Rupert maintained his casual attitude but inside he was shaking. Why had he picked this hotel?

'Yes' - on went the girl 'I always wondered what they did with all that Arts Council money.'

'Oh quite' Rupert drank some of his lager - checked his watch then...'er... is there another dining room?'

'Pardon?' said the girl - now wiping glasses -

'I said - is there another dining room? You see I am not part of the party tonight.'

'Oh - that's alright - there are one or two others here who aren't - we have a separate dining room at the back - it's very nice!'

'Oh - that's all right then' - he was very relieved as he was beginning to feel very hungry...

'Yes they are having their party in the main banquet room - they will probably be dancing later - if I know anything...'

'That usually happens does it?' asked Rupert -

'Oh yes - this is well off the beaten track here - lots of official bodies come here for a rave-up!'

Rupert was about to say something when into the bar came Ianto Price the little solicitor. Rupert was sure that his heart had stopped as the minute lawman looked around the bar - then straight at him - then turned away and looked closely at the barmaid -

'Ah good evening my dear...' his smile reminded Rupert of a baby crocodile - all small teeth and cold wet eyes...

'I'll have a gin and tonic please, love.'

'Yes sir' - the girl was obviously used to this type of man - she placed the drink on the counter in front of the solicitor...

'On the Arts Council bill my love...' said the crocodile as he wandered off towards the windows of the bar and looked out... Rupert found that he had been holding his breath all this time - now he exhaled and took a grateful swallow of his lager and his brain slowly began to work again. Of course the little Brecon lawyer did not recognise him, the man he had met was dead... but - thought Rupert - the Arts Council people who were at the play would know him - but that was not too bad as he was to meet them tomorrow anyway.

He decided, however, to try and keep out of their way as far as possible - so that he could observe what was going on - without having to be involved... He drank the rest of his drink and determined to go into the small town itself and stay away until the party was in full swing - then he would dine and scout around. His head and his heart seemed to return to normal as he walked slowly along the narrow lane that led to the main Town Centre... but he could still not find any connection in his mind between Ianto Price, Iestyn Morris and the Arts Council... except... his heart started to beat faster again - except... Blanchard!

A car came towards him and he had to step on to the grass verge to give room as it passed - he was sure that he recognised the old Brigadier from the Khyber Pass... stranger and stranger... who else was going to be at this party and what was the party all about - and why hadn't he been invited? He liked parties...

Without passing any more cars Rupert reached the Town and walked around for a while checking out the number of pubs and finding the local Theatre - which had some pictures and posters outside - but Rupert could not understand them as the captions were in Welsh. At least he presumed it was Welsh - they may have had a visiting Bengali Dance Company in residence - but he did not think so. After darkness had descended and opening time had elapsed - he picked on one of the smaller pubs and went in for a quiet drink.

Luck - good or bad - has been the subject of poems, curses, stories and novels throughout the ages. It has been described variously as 'the fickle finger of fate', 'a lady', as 'favouring the brave' - it is not to be risked but can be chanced and is certainly tried often - it is said to be connected with black cats, magpies, strange West Country pixies, pavement slab cracks, salt, pins and the kisses of chimney sweeps. It can desert when most required and arrive when least expected - it is also a four letter word, and another one with which it rhymes extremely well leapt into Rupert's mind and almost onto his lips as he entered into the gloom of the public bar of the Three Cocks public house in the Town of Harlech....

The interior of the bar was as dark as a wet November evening, only one small light illuminated the small box shaped room and that shone from what served as a counter at one end, two or three tables were set around the sides and the floor was plain wooden planks. The walls and ceiling were of a uniform tobacco brown, as was the small token window. By the counter was one lone bar stool - at two of the tables sat three or four dark clad men of indiscriminate age - all wearing caps or hats of some nature. They sat silently - pint pots of dark beer in front of them - only their eyes moved to acknowledge the fact that Rupert had entered. They did not speak.

For no reason at all Rupert was terrified; but being unable to back out, as he knew that he would look and - more important - feel so foolish, he walked as casually as he could to the bar counter and perching gingerly on the stool peered into the gloom. Beyond, across a small passage way, he could see that there was another bar - slightly more brightly lit - he could not see much of it as the back of a large barman was obscuring most of the view. Rupert could just see the shoulder of what he presumed to be a customer. The two seemed to be deep in conversation. Rupert coughed - nothing happened - he coughed louder and tapped gently on the counter. The large man turned and looked across at Rupert for what seemed like an hour - then - in a deep, surprisingly North Country accent said:

'Knocking the place down won't get you a drink, friend - wait your turn eh?' He turned back mumbling to the customer. Why - thought Rupert - was he always caught out like this - all he wanted was a quiet drink of lager, and without trying he had managed to put himself in an uncomfortable bar and an embarrassing situation. To calm his nerves and to regain his poise he took out his packet of cigarettes, selected one and flipped open his Zippo lighter, nonchalantly struck the wheel with his thumb and heard the sickening crunch of wheel striking the metal tip of the tension spring... desperately he struck the wheel again but he knew it was no use - even before he saw - in the dim light - the last remnant of the flint fly out and curve away towards the floor.

It is an odd fact that moments of great danger can bring out the very best in people and often they are heard after some great feat of bravery to say that - it was nothing - anyone would have done the same.... and yet other tiny moments of irritation in life can almost destroy people... Thus it was with Rupert...

Being almost blown to bits on the Brecon Beacons had shaken him certainly - but the fact that his lighter had picked this moment to shed its flint - almost pushed him over into gibbering, screaming hysterics. The only thing that stopped him was the flaring match that was hovering near his face - gratefully he dipped the end of his cigarette into the flame and lit it...

'You can never trust them fancy lighters, friend' said the barman discarding the spent match... At the back of his mind Rupert was trying to work out just what those tough American G.I.'s in the second world war did when, in the middle of their mad dashing attack on the stronghold of the entire Japanese army on the beaches of Ippiwana or wherever, their world famous and guaranteed trusty, never-let-you-down or we-give-you-money-back Zippos ran out of flint... 'Yes' was all he said to the barman -

'Will you be wanting a drink then?'

'What? Oh yes...' - In the gloom Rupert tried to see what the barman looked like but apart from the man's bulk could discern little of his face - 'Yes I'll have a pint of lager please...' There was a slight pause, then a great silence descended on the room, a palpable deathly silence, followed by a combined in drawing of breath from the dark men at the tables.... Rupert turned but they were not looking at him - a slight cough brought his attention back to the barman - 'Beg pardon sir' - there was no apology in the tone - 'but this is a real ale house!'

'Oh!' breathed Rupert -

'One of the best known real ale houses in the area. - if not in the country...'

'Ah!'

'If you really want some of that chemical muck, served at a temperature that would freeze the balls off a brass gnu - then I suggest you go up the road to the gin palace they call the Red Lion Hotel - but watch your pockets...'

'Ah - no - not at all' said Rupert wishing he had the nerve to do just that -

'Right then - it will be a pint of real, at blood temperature then?'

'Oh yes, why not' - being a man of the world who had eaten frogs legs, squid and laver bread, Rupert was sure he could handle real ale...

'And a box of matches?'

'Ah yes please!'

While he waited for his pint Rupert scanned the room more carefully. Now that his eyes had adjusted to the gloom he saw that there were pictures in frames around the wall - all depicting - as far as he could gather - famous regiments - all Welsh regiments he imagined. His eyes wandered to the silent ones at the tables - none of them were looking at him nor did they seem to be aware of each other... most odd.

'Seventy pence altogether, sir…'

Rupert turned, in front of him was a tankard type glass of dark foaming liquid - Rupert only liked thin non-handled straight glasses but did not feel up to saying so at this point - beside the pint was a box of England's Glory matches - Rupert was surprised at this, but made no comment. If the barman wished to risk his luck against the Welsh Nationalists that was his problem! He carefully lifted the pint to his lips - sent a mental apology to his hard worked digestive system and took a drink.

In his local pub in West Putney - Rupert's favourite landlord, a wise man of the world who had served in Her Majesty's Navy with distinction as an Able Seaman First Class, had often remarked that people who liked real ale were a strange breed of people, and that they - on the whole - did not spend much but preferred to sip half pints of this insipid soapy slush and discuss steam trains, four-masted schooners or the passing of the Empire - and often collected beer mats. He, the Landlord, had thought of splitting his bar up into two sections - one for real ale and the other for real drinkers. Rupert sat quite still for a few moments after swallowing his first mouthful of the warm, frothy and almost slimy fluid and thought anyone who could habitually drink this stuff must have had their palate removed and stomach lined with pig iron. He could not think of an adjective to express his feelings

'Smashing drop of ale that sir, straight from the wood too...'

To Rupert, it tasted as though it had come straight from the rotten vegetation on the floor of the Belgium Congo rain forests - 'Ah...?'

'You have to look after it properly you know...'

'Yes...' As the man was staring at him Rupert had no choice but to take another drink... 'Ah - yes' he said, as more soap suds fell happily on his stomach. As he was lowering his glass, his eye was attracted by a movement in the other bar and he caught just a glimpse of someone - before the barman turned and his bulk obscured Rupert's view - but it was enough for Rupert to recognise the bulk, receding hair and tinted glasses of the theatre man from Brecon....

Was everyone concerned with his investigation, here in Harlech? Was his whole life directed to this moment in Harlech? What had all this to do with the death of Blanchard? He leaned back as far into the gloom of the bar as he could - in the hope that the Brecon man would not see him - he did not know why but he did not want to be seen by him. He swallowed down the rest of his beer, fear lending easy access to the revolting fluid, picked up his matches and left the pub - as smoothly as he could.

It was only when he was outside and walking in the dark street, thinking about all the people who seemed to be spending tonight in Harlech that a weird truth leapt into his mind. All the time he had been in the Three Cocks back bar - not only had none of the dark men of Harlech sitting at the tables spoken a word - but as he left he saw - without registering the fact at that moment - that none of them had touched their drinks.

11   Of Champagne, Leeks and Death

Rupert blinked - then blinked again - then looked once more to the east - there was no doubt about it - there was a thin streak of light on the far horizon - daylight - glorious - wondrous - miraculous daylight. Not caring whether his would-be killers were near or not Rupert eased himself gingerly out of the bowl of the oak tree, hung by his arms for a few seconds then let himself drop to the ground. His legs - having been cramped in painful positions most of the night - immediately collapsed under him and he went sprawling on his back in the long, damp, cold grass. Despite the cold and wet, Rupert lay back in ecstasy at being able to stretch his legs and relax his back. He did not think that his pursuers would attempt to gun him down in daylight so he felt almost safe for the first time since he had run from the hotel grounds in the middle of the night.

He had left the strange dark world of the Three Cocks and as casually as possible he had strolled up the road until he came to the Red Lion - which looked much more welcoming. Feeling as though the eyes of the previous landlord were boring derisively into his back, he entered the bright interior - a juke box was pumping out the latest hit single by a group Rupert couldn't even pronounce the name of - but it was cheerful and the words did not intrude on the sound. He walked to the bar where one or two local lads were sitting on plastic topped barstools. He caught the attention of the middle aged barmaid, ordered and was served his pint of lager with offhand almost cold indifference - which made him feel distinctly homesick for London. He sat at a table and looked around - apart from the youths at the bar and an earnest couple poring over house for sale handouts - the bar was empty. He relaxed, and as the cool taste of his favourite brand of lager washed away the memory of real soap suds, he contemplated the evening ahead of him. It was obvious that he would have to keep a very low profile and try to find out as much as possible about what was going on in the country hotel.

The fact that so many of the people he had met during his investigations into Blanchard's strange death were now gathered at the hotel on this night led Rupert into thinking that there must be a connection. Was Blanchard in some way connected with this motley group or had he stumbled upon them by chance and discovered that they were up to some crime or other connected with industrial espionage.... or was it something to do with Blanchard's sexual tastes...? Whatever it was, it was all very confusing to Rupert and he imagined that even Bond would have found it difficult to unravel it all at this point, but he at least would have had some beautiful girl in tow by this chapter in the story.

Rupert, realising with disappointment that there was no sex interest in his investigation so far, thought back to the females he had met so far in Wales. No - he thought - there were none that he would have wanted to fill the role of Pussy Galore - although the Director of the best theatre company in Wales could easily have doubled for a SMERSH hit man...

'Ah well' - thought Rupert - it always annoyed him anyway when the females in spy thrillers managed to get in the way of the action....

After having another couple of pints and getting lost on the way back from the pub's loo - he decided it was time to get to work and start finding the answers to all his questions. He walked slowly up the now dark, unlit lane to the Hotel. In the car park there were now far more cars, and light was streaming out of the downstairs dining room. He looked through the glass but the room was empty. The large tables were laid for a very expensive banquet - judging by the number of different glasses set by each place. Before going in Rupert noticed a large laurel bush quite close to the window at one end and decided to come back when the meal was in full swing and conceal himself there and observe the fun...

Cautiously he entered the reception area - but it was deserted. On the counter sat the open register. Rupert looked around to ascertain that there was no-one around and took a look at the book. He recognised one or two of the names and saw that he had been right about the Brigadier - but what surprised him most was that most of them had given their addresses simply as Arts Council Cardiff - and according to the entries most of them had brought their wives with them. This was very puzzling as Rupert was well aware that, although certain movements in London were campaigning and banner-waving for total liberation - as yet there was not a gay wedding service that was recognised by the state...

He was pondering this point when a door adjoining the reception area opened and the sound of a crowd swelled forth, from the bar within, a girl in her twenties came out - she was dressed in the uniform of the arts - a long shapeless dun coloured kaftanish dress hung with brass beads and leather thongs - her hair hung long and straight over her shoulders - - Rupert did not recognise her nor she him - but she came straight up to him.. 'Oh Hello I'm Fiona!' She stuck her hand out at him - being a gentleman he took and shook it -

'Hello' he said -

'You with the party? We are all in there' - she indicated the room from which she had entered -

'Ah no' said Rupert 'just passing through' -

'Oh' said the girl - quite surprised - 'I thought everyone was at the party tonight - it's really smashing.'

'What's it in aid of?' Rupert asked trying to turn on his most charming nature...

'Oh - it's just a party - you know'... She had suddenly become quite cold - almost suspicious - definitely secretive - thought Rupert... She moved off towards the stairs...'Yes - just a party!'

Rupert waited for her to get out of sight and then started to follow her up the stairs to find his own room.

'Can I help you, sir?' Rupert's heart nearly stopped as he turned to face this new threat - but it was only the hotel manager and he was smiling... 'You look a bit lost?'

'Ah well yes, I am a bit... you see I wanted a drink but I don't want to barge in there you know...' - he pointed to the bar...

'Ah - you are not with the party - are you?'

'No - I'm just passing through..'

'Well that's alright - we have another bar round the side which we use when we have big parties - I'll show you...'

Better and better thought Rupert - at least he could have a drink without being discovered - he followed the manager round to the other bar which was situated directly opposite the main bar, but was reached through a separate door and was obscured from sight by a central optics bar. This suited Rupert well as he found that he could hear some of the conversation of the people at the party who were standing drinking near the bar.

The first voice he heard was that of the old Brigadier - leading forth on the falling standards of behaviour in the young nowadays and the increasing cost of the necessities of life such as alcohol, fishing licenses etc. This was not going to get him very far - thought Rupert - but he was wondering just how this old soldier fitted into the scheme of things - he apparently knew the arts people - so - just as he was thinking this thought he heard another voice that he recognised - how could he forget it?

'Large gin and tonic please - hello Uncle George!'

The voice was that of the Lady Director from Cardiff - at the moment she sounded quite sober... Rupert's previous wonderings were made clear to him as he heard the hero of the Royal Engineers answer - 'Good evening my dear, you are looking lovely!' Rupert tried to remember if the old man had worn strong glasses when last he had spoken to him... lovely?

'Thank you uncle - I'm so glad you could make it - we have a few serious problems to sort out this time - thank you...' Rupert realised that the last couple of words must mean that she had just been served her drink..

'Are we all here tonight then?' said the Brig.

'Yes - it's a full meeting and we have the drama panel as well...'

'Umpht' - This was obviously a comment on the arts in general - strange? Rupert's mind was trying to understand - he had thought that this meeting was all arts connected if not then who was 'all of them'?

'What time is the real meeting then, me dear?'

'Midnight - as usual Uncle dear...'

'Good - I'll be able to have a rest after the 'sindig'...' Rupert imagined that the old boy had meant to say 'shindig' but later that night he was not so sure...

'Carol darling...' another voice sailed over to Rupert - it was vaguely familiar but Rupert could not quite place it...

'Ricky darling - I didn't know you were coming...'

'Am I really?' said the famous playwright and then laughed at what was obviously an old and trusted gag -

'Same old script Ricky!'

'Well I would not want to waste my best material on this lot!' Though Rupert could not see him, he imagined that the 'finest young playwright in Wales at the moment' had just indicated the assembled party goers - 'When do we eat and get down to the serious drinking?' the writer continued…

'We are just waiting for our guest of honour to arrive and then we will all go in' answered the Lady Director…

'That old fool! Can't think why he has been invited - his books are rubbish and as boring as hell!'

'Just because he doesn't have people screwing every ten minutes Ricky - you mustn't think that he is dull' - the Director's voice had an icy edge to it - 'he is one of the greatest authorities on Welsh Culture and History...'

'Welsh culture - my my - what a world!' snapped in the writer, 'To most of them good art is a well taken drop-kick - - culture Ha!'

'Mind your manners young man - there are ladies present!' the Brigadier's voice had a tone that must have quelled many a young subaltern - but it had little effect on the boorish word-smith -

'Save that tone for your toy soldiers Brig - the pen is mightier than the sword…' There was a sort of grunt from the Brig and then...'Insubordinate little tyke...'

The writer had apparently moved away, as the next statement from the Director would not have pleased him - 'Don't worry about him Uncle dear - he's had his time as our pet writer - he's out now…'

'Good.' - succinctly from the Brig…

Through the hubbub from the bar Rupert could hear someone banging a glass - then he heard a high pitched female voice...

'Ladies and gentlemen - the Professor has arrived!' There was a smattering of half cheers and some applause - 'so if you would like to make your way to the main dining room we can start on the dinner...' There was a louder sound of approbation at this news and Rupert heard the crowd moving away.

He was about to move away - when he heard the Director speak quietly to the Brig. - 'I hope the old fool enjoys his dinner - it will be his last.' There was a sharp intake of breath then -

'Be careful Carol dear - remember the war time slogan - careless talk can cost lives.'

'Sorry Uncle - it's just that I am nervous - we do seem to have a lot of problems at the moment...'

'I know' replied the Brig - 'but you must stay calm my dear - nothing to be gained by losing your nerve you know...'

'You are right of course - but it's very worrying - three deaths in such a short space of time - someone is bound to get suspicious - aren't they?' This last statement was made quite calmly - Rupert thought - considering the content. He could not hear the Brig's reply as the two were moving away from the other bar.

The young barmaid came round to his side of the bar - she looked harassed - 'Do you want another drink sir?' she asked, 'only I have to help with serving the food in a minute...'

'Yes I will have another lager please.'

Rupert was feeling decidedly queasy. How could these people go into a dinner party so calmly when they were planning murder... at least that was what he supposed they had been talking about... and what was the other meeting at midnight about? Surely this all had to do with his investigation... he felt a chill of fear as he thought of the consequences, if all this was some quite innocent party and that he was in the wrong place altogether - what a fool he would feel - but no, there must be a connection - the little solicitor was here and he had tried, indirectly, to kill Rupert....

'When you are ready, sir?' Rupert nearly fainted as he heard the voice - then he turned and saw that the manager was standing at the door of his small bar.

'Ready?' squeaked Rupert - unable to control his vocal chords...

'For dinner sir' - the manager looked at Rupert puzzled - 'You don't have to look so startled sir, our cooking is not that bad, in fact it is highly recommended' -

'I am sorry' said Rupert - 'I was miles away - you made me jump - yes of course I am ready - lead the way, I must say I am feeling a little hungry...'

This was a gross understatement for, despite his misgivings about his present situation - he was ravenous - he had not eaten since lunch in the pub in Llandovery. How safe and friendly the little town seemed - Rupert doubted if anything ever happened there.... He followed the manager into a small but very chic dining room that had only three dining tables neatly arranged to afford as much privacy to the diners as possible. He was shown to his table and the manager lit a large red candle that was set in a crystal holder - the effect was very romantic - thought Rupert, or would have been if he had not been dining alone…

'I hope you won't feel too lonely on your own sir' said the manager, as he handed Rupert a large leather bound menu - 'We do have another couple staying but they decided not to dine in tonight…'

'Oh - that's all right' answered Rupert 'I will be fine'-

'Good - I'll be back very shortly for your order then…' With that he left the room. Rupert, despite his statement, did feel very lonely and very alone. What kind of people was he dealing with? They were obviously much more powerful than his Boss had imagined - Rupert felt unequipped to deal with the situation but some inner driving force made him resolve to see it through.

As far as he was aware there was no tradition of heroism in his family, his father had served in the medical corps at the end of the last war but had spent most of his time shaving the corns of irate generals. There were no brave sailors, airmen or royal marines in his ancestry, though he did have an Uncle Cyril who was a scout leader in Rickmansworth - but that hardly counted. No, he really could not think how he even came to be contemplating taking on these dangerous people - but he knew he was going to... Bond would not have 'phoned home for help would he? He looked at the menu determined to have a good meal at least, then he felt the hand of fate and the ghosts of long dead squid reaching out for him, the damn thing was all in French - not a sight of a fish and chips anywhere... Racking his brain for any remembrance of his schoolroom French lessons he scanned the offending document. Finally after a desperate search he settled for a simple looking soup as a starter - soupe a l'oignon - which he hoped would be onion of some kind - then as a main course he picked a beefsteak au roquefort - because it vaguely reminded him of a macho T.V. hero. He went for a safe red house wine and another pint of lager.... he did not bother to look at the sweets - as he was trying to watch his weight.

The meal turned out to be the best that he had experienced in Wales - even if the portions were a little on the small side. Rupert had often wondered about this new cooking that seemed to be the rage in London. Now he had seen it. On his plate had been a small piece of steak floating, or so it seemed, in a small lake of sauce and artistically placed around the edge of the plate were a sliced carrot, two sprigs of parsley and a very thinly sliced potato....but it was tasty... and the soup had had real bits of onion floating about in it alongside cubes of toast.... the wine was well behaved and the lager suitably chilled. Yes, altogether it was a pleasant enough dinner. He sat back, lit a cigarette, sipped a brandy and contemplated the night ahead. Sooner or later he would have to screw up his courage and go out and hide in the laurel bush. He had to find out exactly who was at the dinner... It was only now that he thought he ought to have had a small spy type camera.... As he was thinking of this and other things he would have liked, such as a small machine gun, a few hand grenades and maybe a platoon or two of commandos, the noise from the main dining room rose to a soaring crescendo of clapping and cheering, which indicated to Rupert that the point had been reached when most good dinners are ruined by a handful of half-drunk people making inane speeches. Time for him to make a move, before they started breaking up and heading for the bar.

Taking care to check that the hall way was clear he went to his room. He put on his light weight mac - although it would show up in the dark, it would seem he was just going for a walk after dinner - to anyone who just might notice him as he left. Once outside excitement began to take the place of the fear he had been feeling - and after all - surely - nothing really bad could happen to him - could it???

He walked casually down the drive until he thought that he would be out of sight of the windows - then he cut across a narrow grass verge into the deeper darkness and slowly crept back up towards the laurel bush. He reached it without trouble and tucked himself right inside between it and the nearest window of the dining room. Fortunately the curtains of the room had not been drawn too carefully and he was able to see into the room very clearly. From where he was hidden the people at the top table had their backs to him but he could recognise most of them anyway - in the centre and obviously in charge was the Brigadier - beside him sat the Gestapo looking arts man from Cardiff - on his left sat the director lady and next to her the little solicitor - nearest to Rupert was the unmistakeable back view of the old Professor of Welsh History - his long white hair flowing down on his shoulders.

Slowly Rupert tried to identify as many of the others as he could... most were, of course, strangers to him but he could see the two bald eggheads sitting beside each other giggling, several of the long haired kaftanned ladies were there - their hair looking no cleaner than before - Iestyn Morris was leaning over a large breasted girl beside him and leering - his toupee sliding down over his forehead... Down the table beyond a couple of strangers, sat the two police Inspectors Thomas and Evans - they were chatting together as thick as thieves - thought Rupert - or thief-catchers.

He craned as near to the window as he dared but there were still just a few guests that he could not see fully - but even what little he could see showed him that the man from the Brecon Theatre was not among them - strangely, this gave him heart. As he watched, the Gestapo Officer from the Arts Council stood up slightly unsteadily and began making a speech. Rupert could not hear very well but he did catch the odd phrase that was obviously spoken at a higher volume... such as... 'A great year for the arts in Cardiff... Wonderful new venture.... Totally new concept in theatre...' He seemed to end with almost a Hitleresque type salute and a shout of - 'More theatre for Cardiff!' He then fell back into his chair amid cheers and clapping from the assembly... Rupert did notice that the Brig and the little solicitor were not looking very pleased or indeed very interested in this performance.

Suddenly, as though on a hidden signal, people began getting up - some were moving toward the door - while others were moving the tables about - obviously the 'sindig' was about to begin.... Rupert backed away from the windows and into the shadows - for once luck seemed to be moving his way for as he faded into the deeper darkness around the laurel bush the front door of the hotel opened and several of the guests spilled out noisily into the car park shouting to each other and obviously feeling the heat as one girl had thrown off her cardigan. Rupert hoped that she was not going to go any further - there was a limit to his nerve and the sight of any of these arty women without their coverall mini tents would surely drive him over the edge.

Happily there was no need to panic as the girl was only putting her cardy in a car nearby... Rupert knew she called it a cardy as he heard her shout to a friend: 'Hang on I am just going to put my cardy in the car...' Other guests had come out onto the steps in front of the hotel and were milling about - smoking and drinking... Rupert - although he had not been outside very long - developed a great thirst and a longing for a smoke.... he was too far away from the group to hear any of their conversation and in any event they were not the important ones to him - he assumed that they were all the so called 'Drama Panel.' - they looked sufficiently arty!

From inside the dining room came the sound of pop music played loud - Rupert looked in from where he stood and saw that the tables had been cleared away and a space was now available for dancing. Indeed several people were already throwing themselves about with gay abandon - Rupert assumed it was gay abandon as most of the couples were of the same sex....

He waited until the people who had come outside returned to the party and then carefully walked back inside and made it to the private back bar without encountering any of the opposition - as he now thought of them... He had a drink and settled down as near to the bar as possible to try and catch what conversation he could from the other side - but there was nothing much of interest as most of the crowd were in the main dining room dancing or swigging back the champagne, which Rupert had noticed through the window was in plentiful supply - but he did overhear a husband and wife type row between two of the men, one of whom he recognised from his whining voice as an actor in the play he had seen in Cardiff... something was going wrong with the relationship - according to the whiny one the other was being unfaithful with a director or something... Rupert felt a bit guilty about listening and wondered why, whenever Bond was in this sort of situation the conversation would be between two of the enemy and concern the plans for the destruction of the world - which only he, Bond, could now stop - thanks to having overheard them, but - now all Rupert heard was 'You are just being a silly bitch Brian - once he's used you - you will be out - you know that...'

'And you are just jealous Kevin, I know about you and him and the Jacuzzi - he told me...'

'Oh well - just don't come crying to me when he throws you aside that's all... two gins and tonic please!'

Rupert was fascinated but knew that it did not help his task - though he thought he vaguely recognised the other voice.... At that point the barmaid popped her head round the corner to his bar - he declined another drink but thought it amazing how she seemed to know just when his glass was empty - he didn't notice the mirror situated over the bar on her side....

From the noise emanating from the banqueting room the party was obviously getting into full swing... a good time to get to his room thought Rupert, and wait for midnight and what he felt in his bones was going to be the climax to this investigation... He turned to go towards the bar door and so didn't notice the look on the face of the barmaid - which was a pity because she quite obviously fancied him and although he never knew it, she would quite happily have provided all the sex interest for his assignment that he could have wished for... as it was he went out of the door without the slightest suspicion that there was the chance of a very different night ahead - a night a great deal more pleasant than the one he was quite innocently about to embark upon....

12   A touch of the Megans in the Night

Rupert lay half-awake beneath the tall old oak tree that had been his refuge during the long autumn night. Life was returning to his legs - he was very cold and this made him remember his coat - he turned over onto his stomach and looked towards the hedge where he had thrown the garment early in the night. It was still there spread out like a one dimensional scarecrow on the hedgerow. He pulled his knees up beneath him and started to get up - intending to get the coat and then to find a road and look for some help. He was on his feet leaning against the tree for support when the high-pitched nasal voice stopped his heart -

'Rupert - dear boy - where have you been hiding all night?' Rupert froze - which was not difficult as he had been near to zero temperature to start with - he turned - they were standing about eight feet away, both were wearing flat caps, army type camouflage jackets, jeans and large wellies - both carried nasty looking double barrelled shot guns which at the moment were pointed at Rupert's most vulnerable spot.... Rupert did not know much about guns - he knew how to point them and what to pull of course, but he was quite sure that either barrel of either of these two guns contained enough power to send his parents into mourning for the second time in a month. The man who had spoken lifted the gun until it was levelled at Rupert's heart...

'We are so sorry you have to leave us Rupert dear - but Megan says you have to go and she must be obeyed - mustn't she? Goodbye love! '

The other man sniggered as the first man's finger started to whiten on the trigger. In the seconds left to him Rupert would have liked to have remembered all the good things that had happened to him - all the girls, the drinks - and made some witty last remarks - but all that went through his mind was - Why me? It's not fair! Help! Not all his past life flashed through his mind as he had been told it did - only a small fraction of it...

He remembered leaving the small bar last night and making his way to his bedroom. On the way he had seen a few of the party-goers lolling about in odd alcoves at various levels of intoxication and various stages of undress. In the corridor leading to his room two totally naked men were leaning against the wall - each holding a champagne bottle and a glass and talking most earnestly with the myopic intensity that typifies the drunk. Rupert hesitated for a second when he recognised one of them as the actor who had played the main part in the play in Cardiff and who earlier had been having a row in the bar. He wondered if the other one was Brian - happily neither of the two took any notice of him and he went into his room without trouble...

From his room he could hear the noise of the party - voices were raised in song - there were snatches of 'Bread of Heaven' a well-known song about a saucepan and 'Abide with Me' sailing out into cold Welsh night air... Also, Rupert heard the sound of breaking glass... Did the Welsh have the Russian habit of throwing their glasses into the fireplace he wondered - or were they just so drunk that they couldn't hold their glasses let alone their drink?

Rupert lay on his bed and let the sounds filter up to him as he tried to rest and get the facts in order before midnight. Suddenly there was a crash from outside his room followed by a cry and some good English swearing - a woman's voice shouting... Rupert got off the bed, turned off his light and ventured to open the door a little to see what was causing the row. Just down the corridor slightly beyond the two naked men who were still totally wrapped up in each other - was the Lady Director from Cardiff and a very drunk author - the Director was up against the wall - being held there by the author, who seemed determined to find a way up the inside of her kaftan - she was pulling his hair trying to stop him… she was shouting at him at the same time..

'For God's sake Rick… I am not in the mood… can't you understand…'

'Come on - you bitch - I was good enough for you last week...' he dived down and tried to pull her dress up again... Rupert pulled his door shut unable to bear the sight any longer. He sat back on his bed and pondered on the strangeness of the human race - here was this little writer - whose play Rupert had seen and hated for its total lack of drama, style or plot - showing courage that would have won him a V.C. during the war… Rupert shuddered… There was more shouting from outside then the slamming of doors...a degree of quiet descended - softer music drifted up from the dining room - Rupert saw that it was getting near to midnight. Where, he wondered, was the secret meeting to be held and how was he to get near enough to hear or see what was going on? What would Bond have done? By this time, of course, he would have infiltrated into the gang disguised as a bona fide buyer from an import-export firm in Hong Kong - he would even have had his face disguised by a make-up artist from H.Q. to look like a genuine Indian skinhead or whatever... well at least he - Rupert - had had his hair dyed - but he was no nearer the centre of this mystery.

With the room still in darkness Rupert went to the window and looked out - not for any reason just to think... and while he was staring out over the car park he thought he noticed something white and large moving across the lawn and into the wood opposite. He blinked, thinking that he had probably been imagining things - then he looked again - this time there could be no mistake - there was a figure similar to the first moving slowly across the lawn - it seemed to be wearing a hooded white sheet - it too crossed the grass and disappeared into the wood... Could this be what he had been waiting for - could this be at long last a break... if so then it was heaven sent? How should he take advantage of this gift?

As he was thinking, yet a third figure quickly crossed over the verge and entered the woods. Rupert made up his mind - he would go into the woods and find out where these people were going. He wondered if, like his hero, he should grab a sheet and try to infiltrate as a member of the sect whatever it was. He had to dismiss this idea when he discovered that the sheets on his bed were of the rainbow coloured striped variety... the best he could do - he thought - was to wear his white mac and hope that no-one saw him crossing the lawn.

He stepped out of his room. The corridor was now empty - he went down the stairs into the reception area - he could still hear music but there was no-one in sight. He walked quickly out of the front door - hesitated for a moment or two then taking his courage in both hands stepped out towards the grass verge and the wooded area opposite. There were no shouts and no shots - which was much more important to Rupert. He reached the edge of the woods and the place where he judged that the figures had entered - looked once more behind him and sending up a silent prayer he plunged in. It was very dark but he could just make out a sort of path leading deeper into the woods. He tried to keep to the side as much as possible in best jungle warfare fashion, keeping a look-out behind him at the same time. He moved in this fashion slowly for about five minutes then he saw that the path widened out and he could see quite clearly that there was a building up ahead. It looked in the dark like a typical Welsh barn painted white... Rupert paused a few yards away not sure of how he should get into the place. This was lucky for him as his stillness enabled him to hear the sounds of someone else approaching from behind. Taking a deep breath to try and stop his heart beating so fiercely he moved quickly into the cover of the darkness of the wood off the path. He was not a moment too soon as down the path came a further hooded figure - it passed his hiding place without pausing - breathing heavily under its hood - it moved hurriedly across the clearing and went round to the right hand side of the barn type building. Rupert did not hesitate but left his cover and dodged round the corner in time to see the figure entering through a small doorway. He waited a second and then approached the opening - there was a dim light and he could see into a sort of vestibule, the back of the cloaked figure was going through another door into a more brightly lit room. When the door had shut behind it Rupert crept into the small anti-room. Either side of him he saw that there were flights of stairs curving away into the dark - he did not have time to make any decision as he heard the unmistakeable sound of more people arriving - he dived to his left and as quietly as he could he went up the stairs until he considered that he was completely hidden in the darkness. Luck was still with him it seemed, for as soon as he had stopped moving two more figures came in through the door and shut it behind them. Rupert heard the sound of a bolt being pulled across - so these were the last!

There was a brief moment of panic when the two figures opened the door to the main room and light spilled out - Rupert felt sure that he could be seen but the two were not looking in his direction, and to his relief they went in and the door shut behind them. When he felt quite sure that there were no more hooded creatures to come, he started to edge his way very slowly up the stairs - he did not have far to go before he came to what he assumed by the flatness in the darkness - was a landing - and to his left and low down near the floor he could just discern a thin, line of light... very, very carefully he moved toward it and when he was close he could just make out the thin outline of a door - from behind which he could hear the faint buzz of voices. He found the handle of the door, so he deduced, hoping that he was right, this must lead to some sort of gallery - with any luck and if he could get in undetected he might be able to witness whatever was going on... He turned the handle - it moved smoothly, then he gave an experimental tug - the door moved towards him... The spirit of Bond was with him tonight... he smiled in the dark. Then, on the basis that this was in fact a gallery, he dropped to the floor and lying flat he opened the door a fraction at a time and peered in - hoping that no eyes were at this moment fixed on the moving door... Soon it was open wide enough for him to crawl into the room, but before moving he waited... the murmur of voices rose up to him but there was no sign that his opening the door had been noticed - so in his best imitation of a crawling commando he edged himself in.

He had been right about it being a gallery - it was very narrow - not more than four or five feet, but was high enough for anyone not actually leaning over the railing to be unseen from the floor of the hall... or as Rupert realised quite quickly - the Chapel - for that undoubtedly was what it had been - one of the very small chapels that had sprung up during the years of rebellious non-conformist breakaway churches. Most of them were now disused and derelict or had been converted to studios by incoming English potters and painters. Rupert slid towards the rail, wanting to get a good look into the room... The light was all in the main hall and the gallery was only dimly lit by the spillage upwards... He reached the edge safely and looked down....

During the preceding days Rupert had known moments of fear, even he had to admit to himself moments of near panic, he had felt his heart stop, he had had his blood freeze - he had been at one point close to screaming hysterics - but what he felt now, as he stared from the merciful shadows, down into the main well of this one time chapel - did things to his mind and body that would be of great interest to any aspiring doctor - hoping to specialise in psychiatry He shut his eyes and tried to pretend that he was not really here - opened them and found he was - he tried swallowing hard to stop his heart from leaping out of his mouth and down into the room - it seemed to work partially - and he desperately wanted to pee...

The thought that at this most traumatic moment of his young life - the thought uppermost in his mind was having a pee, was almost the ruin of Rupert, but he somehow managed to stifle the rising burst of hysterical laughter and looked once more onto the scene spread out below him.

It was not a large room - the walls were painted white the same as the outside. All the windows had been boarded over with wooden panels on which were painted pictures of what seemed to be medieval characters - all performing some kind of violent act - one was slashing at a man with a sword, another was setting fire to a pile of faggots packed around a priestly looking gent - yet another was putting a noose around the neck of a woman on a scaffold - all were painted in the bright primary colours associated with the medieval period. Rupert turned his eyes away from these grisly murals and looked at the scene in the room.

In the centre was a long refectory table at both ends of which was set an ornate but electric candelabra - each with six electric candles - these provided all the illumination in the hall. In the centre of the table, set neatly on a gold cushion were three objects that confirmed all Rupert's fears and suspicions... an inflated rugby ball was lying in a slight hollow and on one side was a large shiny prize quality leek and on the other - a mint condition copy of Under Milk Wood by Dylan Thomas...

Around the table sat six figures - two on either side and one at each end - all in white hooded robes - only their eyes were visible through narrow slits in the cloth. As Rupert was trying to take all this in, the figure at the end of the table furthermost from Rupert raised his hand and there was silence. The lights dimmed to almost darkness and the hooded figure spoke - Rupert recognised the voice of the Brigadier but it was the words that puzzled him... after all the Brig was just about as English as they came... yet here he was burbling out these anti-English statements in this weird ritual... Rupert could not remember it all as it droned on - but there were things like... 'May all who tread the plank fall foul of those who hold the end' and 'Let all walk over us until they perish in the stormy seas' and 'May all Sais perish in their own arrogance'...

It was a meaningless jumble as far as Rupert could make out but all the others at the table responded with what sounded like 'Yes, yes' after each incantation... Finally the three items on the table were reverently passed around and each member kissed each one in turn until they were all returned to the centre. Rupert could now see that the cushion itself was set on what looked like a rough-hewn plank - the colour of which so blended with the table that Rupert had missed it at first. When everything was back in place the Brig spoke again - this time in a quiet more every-day voice...

'Welcome fellow Tadgis - I will not waste time tonight - as you are aware there are one or two troublesome problems we have to deal with - all of them, may I say, arising from the actions taken by and authorised by Tadgi Three of the Megan Section...' There was a sort of snort from one of the hooded figures on the left of the Brig...

'Tadgi One - I wish to deny that all the blame be placed on my section' - it was the voice of Iestyn Morris - Rupert could see that he was twisting his false hand round and round in agitation... a female voice sang out -

'It was the Megans who committed that silly act on the Beacons' -

'That was a mistake' piped in the Cardiff member of D.I.E.

'Whatever the reason' said the Brig 'it has led us to our present trouble. As you know thanks to your actions another of your Company's employees has been killed - your Bosses are not stupid - they will have set up some sort of investigation' -

Another voice joined in - Rupert recognised this one as the lawyer Ianto Price from Brecon -

'At least we did not commit the idiocy of putting the sacred symbols of the Sons of Ogmore with the body' -

'From what I heard there would be little point' - the voice of the female Director said 'there was none of it to be found' -

The Brig came in again firmly 'Tadgi Four did the best he could do in the time - and is a credit to the Bronwyn Section.'

'I thank you Tadgi One' spoke up the little lawyer - 'I did only what I had to' -

A deep Welsh voice mumbled - 'The little pansy was asking too many questions - nosy bastard he was...'

Rupert realised that this was the Police Inspector from Brecon and that he was drunk or if not, well on the way to being so. He wondered if even Bond had ever overheard his death being discussed after the event. It made Rupert feel very strange indeed - but now he knew the answers - or some of them. He stopped thinking and went back to listening to the meeting - 'But there is another man prowling around now - that berk who was at the theatre the other night' said the Director -

'Nothing to do with my department love' chipped in Morris 'least not as far as I know - they did say someone would be coming down but I haven't been in the office lately...'

'Might have been more help if you had spent more time there' - the Brig sounded fierce and angry -

'Alright - alright' mumbled Morris - 'None of us is perfect you know - I've had problems at home see?' He seemed to sink into his chair and Rupert could imagine the look on his face...

'With respect Tadgi One...' the remaining member of the six spoke for the first time - and it came as no surprise to Rupert to hear the voice of the Police Inspector from Cardiff - 'The fact that our fellow Tadgi left the sacred symbols of our order lying about in his office while he was away screwing some other man's wife or whatever - is unfortunate - but it happened. What has taken place since is unfortunate - but we the Tadgis must sort it out -

our grandchildren in the order expect us to be beyond petty squabbles - don't you think?' He spoke with great authority and seemed to be more in charge than the Brig - thought Rupert - so that is what happened then - poor old Blanchard had stumbled on these symbols of the sons of Ogmore and then?...

The sound of the Brig's voice once more cut across Rupert's thinking - 'You are right to bring us to order Tadgi Six - as you say we have a job to do - this troublesome Professor?'

'I say he has to be silenced' clipped in the Brecon lawyer -

'I agree' said the female Director 'from the description of the man who was with him last week there can be no doubt that it was this Vivian Williams from London - the Grandchild who works at the university says they were together for some time and we know that the old man is nearly ready to publish' -

'Very well' the Brig said 'and this could be the chance for the Megan Section to redeem its good name' -

There was no response from Tadgi Three - Morris was slumped forward over the table - asleep...

'We will tell him later' said the Director -

'Now to the matter of tomorrow Tadgi Two' said the Brig -'Ah yes?'

She got no further for at this point the good luck that had been seeming to sit on Rupert's shoulder this night decided - quite without warning - that she had a prior engagement elsewhere and left - leaving Rupert in the most dreadful panic as he realised that he could no longer control his intense desire to relieve himself. He began to inch his way back towards the door - with the intention of going outside - finding a quiet spot - doing what had to be done and returning to the meeting. His thoughts as he attempted this manoeuvre were of his secret agent hero who seemed never to need to go anywhere near a bathroom unless it was to unscrew his safety razor, take out a complete mini radio, call home and go back into the fray....

Rupert made it to the door turned and pushed it open and crawled out onto the landing - but there disaster struck - the screws that had been holding the hinges of the door must have been on their very last legs, for although they had held when Rupert had first pulled the door open, two movements were obviously two too much for them - there was a sort of soft tearing sound followed by a dull thump as the door dropped off the hinges - then a good loud whump as it toppled and fell onto the small landing beyond the gallery.... Three things then happened almost simultaneously - the lights on the table were turned up to full brightness - the policeman from Cardiff yelled 'There's some bastard in the gallery' and Rupert wet himself....

Then chaos ensued with the two policemen running up the stairs and grabbing Rupert who was unable to defend himself on account of his embarrassing situation. He was man-handled down into the main room and pushed up against a pillar and tied to it... only when this was done did anyone speak... it was the Female Director who broke the silence -

'Well, well, well...' she sneered, 'our little pansy berk from the Arts Council...'

Rupert squirmed, not so much at being called a pansy - or a berk - but because he was still wetting himself... this most definitely never happened to any fictional agents - not even the up-market anti-hero types called Palmer or Bernard... the only saving grace of the whole awkward, not to say dangerous, situation was that he was wearing his black trousers and the damp would not be showing too much. As it happened no-one seemed to notice his problem at all - they had other things on their mind it seemed -

'You know this person Tadgi Two?' the Brig made it sound like an order more than a question -

'Yes Tadgi One' replied the Director 'this is the phony arts man that was dumped on us the other night at the premiere of Rick's play' - she moved in close to Rupert as though staring hard at him - he could just see her piggy eyes through the slits -

'The one you invited to meet the Drama Panel?' said the Brig -

'That's right - but he was not meant to be here until tomorrow' - she poked at Rupert with her index finger 'were you - you silly little pansy?'

Something snapped inside Rupert - he did not know for sure what caused this to happen - it could have been the amount of lager he had drunk or the fact that for the first time since he had been a baby he had wet himself - or fear - mostly though he thought that it was that he was sick and tired of being called gay throughout this assignment - whatever it was he felt certain things had to be said - no matter the consequence -

'Listen to me - you - you - power mad zombies - once and for all I am not gay - nor for that matter am I from the Arts Council - I am an agent of the Department of Industrial Espionage - sub section C.E.S.S. P/OO/L - my name is Rupert Courtney Morgan and I did not die on the Brecon Beacons - no thanks to you... I know all about your mad schemes now and I am not alone - my men know where I am and if anything happens to me they will get you in the end...'

Regretting the grammar and the appalling syntax he burst into tears. No-one in the room moved, nothing broke the silence except the gulping sobs of Rupert as he tried to control himself at both ends. It seemed to him to take forever, but at last he was under control. He looked up - still no-one had moved and now the silence was complete - suddenly...

'It wasn't anyone else's wife you know - it was my greyhound Rosie' - shouted the one handed man from Cardiff -

The even deeper silence that met this remark caused him to sit up and look around the table - noticing that the others were not sitting but all standing at one end of the room and turned towards him he jumped to the wrong conclusion and also burst into tears -

'Listen, just because of one silly mistake - you can't punish me - you can't - it's not fair...' he buried his head in his hands and sobbed on -

The others all moved to the table and sat in their places - the silence continued - finally it was broken by the Brig.

'This is appalling' - he paused... no-one else responded - 'There has never been such a breach of our Councils in the whole history of the Society' - he looked up at Rupert - 'I take it it was you who spoke to the Professor?' - Rupert nodded - 'and he told you what he had found out about our order?'

'Yes - everything - and I told my superiors' - Rupert lied -

'Did you now...' the Brig was silent again for a few moments -

'Whatever the Professor may have said Tadgi One' - it was the Female Director who spoke - 'Only this little interfering bastard can tie it all together you know!'

The Brig looked at her as did the rest of them except Morris who was still crying quietly to himself - The

Policeman from Cardiff spoke - 'You are right Tadgi Two - what the Professor knows is only conjecture on his part and conjecture is not evidence..'

'Quite right Tadgi Six' from the Director. 'Even if our little friend here did tell his bosses and there is only his word that he did... if he did, they still have no proof!'

'That is correct Tadgi Two'. The Brig looked towards Rupert who was now sufficiently recovered to be aware that things were not looking too healthy for him. 'So', continued the Brig 'if we assume that he did inform his bosses we need not really worry - and if not - well?....' He left the question in the air -

'Either way Tadgi One' said the Policeman from Cardiff - 'if he is removed properly and permanently this time, we have only to keep very quiet for a period and no-one will be any the wiser...'

'And the Professor?' - The question came from the Brig -

'Well it would have been better of course if we could have removed him as planned, but now - well I don't think we can risk it... at least not this time...'

'You are right Tadgi Six' said the Brig as he looked around the table, 'are we all agreed?' -

There was a murmur of assent from all - except again poor Iestyn Morris who was now fast asleep -

'There is just one point I would like to make...' This was said by the Brecon Lawyer - who had not spoken in the debate so far - 'And that is - supposing that this spy was telling the truth and that he is not working alone - won't his companions be looking for him?'

This thought had crossed Rupert's mind - after all he had been told that he would be covered at all times. He also thought that this would be an ideal moment for his cover - whoever they were - to come leaping in yelling

'Hands up, don't move, you are all under arrest' - but all that did happen was that the Brigadier summed up the problem all too neatly for Rupert's taste -

'That has occurred to me Tadgi Four - and if what you say were true - then I would have thought that by now they would have been banging down the doors and rushing in yelling 'put your hands up or whatever - what?' - He allowed himself a small laugh -

'You are right as usual Tadgi One' said the small lawyer from Brecon - 'so then it only leaves us with the er... how shall I put it... the modus operandi?'....

'If you mean how do we kill him, why don't you just say so?' said the Brig sharply -

'How do we do it then?' piped in the Director Lady... There was a long pause - Rupert began to think that maybe they would not come up with a suitable idea and forget the whole thing - but no such luck... Typically it was one of the policemen who came up with the simplest of ideas... 'Tadgi One?' - it was the Cardiff Inspector - 'I think the simplest solution would be for our young friend here to have a shooting accident while he is out with a couple of friends - hunting rabbits or pigeon - that sort of thing happens all the time...'

'And the ritual - Tadgi Six?' - this from the Lawyer -

'That can take place here, but the artefacts burned and not placed on the body. I have thought for a long time that that is a dangerous practise and this whole set of problems seem to prove me right...'

'Pinky and Perky can do it' said the Director from Cardiff - 'they enjoy these things' - she gave a shudder under her robe...

'Very well - it is settled then' the Brig moved over to where Rupert was tied - 'You have been a very foolish young man Mr Morgan and now you must pay the price that all who meddle with the sons of Ogmore suffer...' he glared at Rupert for a moment or two and then went toward the door - speaking as he left... 'I am going to bed now - I am getting too old for these rituals - I will send our two friends over in ten minutes - be as quick as you can' - so saying he left.

'Wake Tadgi Three up will you - he might as well see the end of the trouble he has caused...' The two policemen got up at the Female Director's words and went over to Iestyn Morris and began to shake him awake - 'What's the matter - what are you doing?' he mumbled almost incoherent -

'It is time for the ritual of death Tadgi Three' said the Brecon Inspector. The effect of his words were amazing - the little representative of D.I.E. from Cardiff went quite crazy - he leapt up onto the table - tore off his robe and threw it at the two policemen, the force of his yanking off the garment also dislodged the dark toupee which fell onto the head of the female director - at the same time Morris was screaming - 'No you can't do this to me... not the ritual.... not just for one tiny error... that's not fair...' he accidently kicked the rugby ball which flew into the face piece of the lawyer's robe - he twitched backwards and fell off his chair clutching the ball, as his feet came up they caught under the table causing it to tilt just enough to topple the already unsteady Iestyn Morris off and onto the two policemen who fell in a heap beneath him - at the same time the Lady Director was leaning across the table screaming - 'The plank - the plank - don't damage the plank...' - as if it had a life of its own, the said plank leapt in the air - kicked by the falling foot of Morris and struck the Director a sharp blow under the hood - she screamed again, fell and disappeared under the table...

Rupert had been so absorbed by the whole amazing comedy that he had been straining forward against his bonds - suddenly they broke and his own momentum hurled him into the struggling mass on the floor. With any other group he would not have had the chance to escape but the fact that all these people were wearing hooded robes gave him his moment - as the hoods had apparently moved over the eyes of the swearing bundle of arms and legs...

Rupert leapt to his feet and headed for the door like a contender for the hundred metre gold medal fun run - he was through the first door and halfway to the outer door when one of the bald headed double-act appeared in the opening. Rupert did not even break his stride - he went full tilt at the egg-head bowling him over - and through the doorway. Suddenly he was outside and there was the other shiny pated man - he just stared at Rupert who yelled 'Good night Baldy!' and ran like hell into the woods.

He could hear a great deal of shouting going on behind him and he knew they would be after him as soon as they got themselves sorted out and he had no illusions as to what they would do to him when they did catch him. They might seem like a comic set up, but they had killed Blanchard and had tried to kill him - Rupert - once already.

All these thoughts gave his legs wings and he ran and ran. Soon he was somehow out of the woods and crossing fields - falling over hedges - into ditches. He lost all track of time or direction until finally he fell exhausted to the ground. Then the rain came, followed by the force ten hurricane winds. He crawled on until he literally banged into the trunk of a tree - he stood up and tried to shelter from the wind but there was no escape....

He opened his eyes... there they were... the two egg-heads... the shot guns pointed at his heart... he saw the finger of the nearest one tighten on the trigger - he closed his eyes said a last goodbye to all his friends back in London - heard a loud bang and - fainted.

13   Take it easy Mr Morgan

So it was all true! It must be true! Rupert could hear the angels - they were singing softly, gently and in glorious harmony - it did not seem at all incongruous to Rupert that they should be singing the nuns chorus from the Sound of Music. He opened his eyes - yes he was right - everything was white as it should be - bright shafts of light were flashing through the whiteness - well that would be right too... Yes, it was wonderful that this was happening to him just as his Sunday School Teacher had said it would... up through the white clouds into the bright lights of heaven… the Great Gates and then -

Rupert shut his eyes to cut off the picture - the gates - he would have to give an account of his life to the angels - he would have to confess - he started to cry... and tried to speak but all that would come out was a childish voice whimpering - 'I did not mean to kill the budgie, honest mummy, it was an accident - honest...'

'Rupert - come on old chum - you're alright now...' The voice was familiar - slowly his conscious mind surfaced and he opened his eyes again and, a miracle, he was in a hospital bed - a snow white hospital bed - in a snow white hospital room - the early winter sun was streaming through the slats of a Venetian blind covering the window - somewhere a radio was playing. He lifted his head and there sitting at the end of the bed, with a fresh pint of lager in his hand was the Theatre man from Brecon.

Rupert blinked several times and shook his head as it all came flooding back to him... then before he could stop himself he blurted out - 'Where am I? What happened?' - he knew he was alright for he felt an idiot as soon as he heard himself speak the words... The man from Brecon was laughing...

'Well - that's better - I was beginning to get worried about you. Here!' He leaned forward and offered the pint to Rupert, 'take it easy now - you have had a rough ride Rupert old chap - but all is well now and you are a hero you know!'

Rupert sat up and took the lager - took a sip and his dream of heaven returned... he leaned back...

'A hero - but...' he tried to say something else but the Brecon man spoke first -

'A hero I said and a hero I mean' - he produced another lager from the floor and took a drink... 'You have broken up a particularly nasty cell of a very unpleasant organisation - whose sole object is the corruption and ultimate destruction of the fabric of the society...'

'The sons of Ogmore - I remember' said Rupert.

'Oh - that was just a blind' continued the Brecon Man, 'most of them were English drop-outs using the pretext of nationalism for their own criminal ends!'

'Gosh!' said Rupert and wished he hadn't, 'but what were they up to exactly?' he asked, because although he had been all through the assignment he still had no idea what had been going on.

'Same old thing - old mate - money of course. This particular cell had spent a lot of time infiltrating the arts organisation - they were on the point of pulling off quite a coup with a big grant for a non-existent drama company... but you scotched all that...' he took another drink -

Rupert was unable to help saying 'Gosh' again - but he didn't mind really - then he asked - 'Who are you then? I mean really - how do you fit in to all this?'

'Me?' said the Brecon Man - 'I am who I say I am - I really do run a real theatre near Brecon - I have been trying to get grants for ages and I knew there was something fishy going on but I couldn't get close - then I met your Boss' -

'My Boss?' said Rupert - who despite all his adventures still could not stop himself repeating other people... 'You mean?' he added - just to stay in character -

'Yes' said the Brecon Theatre Man - 'A funny little chap with a toy cat and a Russian lady driver...'

'That's him!' said Rupert, 'but how? - I mean - I don't… he knew he was fully recovered now...

'It was after I had spoken to you at the Theatre - we must have been spotted together by your cover. The following day your Boss came to see me and asked me to keep an eye on you - I was only too pleased… '

Rupert thought about this for a moment - then...

'But how did you know my name was Rupert - the night before?'

'Oh - I didn't - it's just that Rupert is my favourite character in fiction, and when I am drunk I tend to call everyone Rupert - Rupert!'

'Oh!' said Rupert - and was about to add more when the door of the room opened and in came his Boss - complete with cat...

'Ah Morgan - so you are awake at last - good!' - he walked over and perched himself on the bed and examined Rupert carefully.

'Well - you look to be fully recovered' - he turned to the Brecon Man - 'How does he sound to you, Simon?' So that was the Brecon Man's name - thought Rupert -

'I hope you have thanked Simon, Rupert - you owe him your life - if he had not spotted you in that hotel in Harlech and rung us we would never have found you in time - as it was, it was touch and go!'

'I didn't know' he looked over to Simon - 'I don't know what to say' -

'Then don't say anything - I was glad I was in time!'

'But I still don't see how they found me - whoever '

'S.A.S.' said his Boss, 'as soon as we found out that you had gone up to Harlech a day early we contacted them immediately, we knew we were dealing with a ruthless group after Blanchard and the firing range affair... They found you just as those two laddies were about to gun you down...'

'Gosh!' said Rupert - it was all so amazing that he could not be bothered to say anything else - 'What has happened to the group then?'

'Well those two are dead - I am afraid the S.A.S. had no choice at that distance - as for the others they are all under arrest... '

'So you see you are a hero Rupert!' said Simon, the Brecon Man -

'Well - not really - I mean it was Blanchard who got onto them first - after all... '

'Blanchard was a fool!' said Rupert's Chief - 'He was onto nothing - except the boy he had taken back to our office in Cardiff - because his landlady was getting suspicious about his friends. He stumbled on those ridiculous artefacts, asked Iestyn Morris about them... and that was that! Morris panicked as the coup was near - and there you have it... '

'Oh!' said Rupert - but inside he did feel quite happy... 'Look sir, I am feeling quite well now - when can I get back to London?'

'You are in London' said the new found friend Simon - 'this is a private ward of the Putney General Hospital' -

'Yes' said the Chief, 'we thought it best to get you out of Wales as quickly as possible - the big boys from the M.I. Sections are mopping up down there...' He paused for a moment then - 'You did very well you know Morgan - a lot of compliments coming the Department's way... and yours...' - he tailed off and went to look out of the window - 'It would seem a pity to waste all the special training and you do have experience now...'

What was the old boy trying to say? thought Rupert. The Chief turned back from the window and after looking at Rupert for a few seconds or so said - 'That Professor chap sends his regards to you - amazing fellow - not a bit worried about being nearly murdered in his bed. Oh - sends his thanks to you too - of course - most grateful!' He is trying to tell me something - thought Rupert -

'Look Rupert - '

This was a bad sign - thought Rupert - the Boss had never used his Christian name before - he waited... 'The thing is' - the Chief wandered around the room as he spoke 'the Professor was most excited that his theory about there being a kind of Tafia in existence has been proved to be fact - he is bringing out his book on the subject quite soon you know...'

Rupert wished that he would get to the point even though in his bones he knew he was not going to like it...

'Well - I will get to the point...' - he stroked the cat for a moment 'and that is - that now we know that these people exist - we can try to combat them... but they are clever - according to the Prof they infiltrate all walks of life at the administrative level and manipulate the finances - like that little lot in Wales...' He came close to Rupert's bed now - he was smiling - 'So for some reason that I am not privy to - though it might have something to do with your success on this last mission' - Rupert liked the way he said 'mission' - 'The Powers that Be have decided that our Department should be the one to spearhead operations, as it does often involve our special interests - and that we should train a few specialist agents for the field - well of course - you qualify for the job - what is more you are already trained' - Rupert could tell that the crunch was coming - 'And there is a problem which may have some connection with these chaps - there have been a couple of strange deaths in a top security electronics firm in Watford...'

Electronics sounded exciting - thought Rupert - though he did not see how he would be much use - he could only just wire a plug - providing the little cardboard guide card was still attached...

'According to the Professor you know - even the English 'sections' - as they are called - of the Tafia - have a Megan sub section who are usually used to do the killing'

Rupert started to worry - after all he had been very lucky to get away with his life once - he didn't fancy risking his luck again...

'Yes' continued the Chief 'something akin to the Russian's SMERSH - even tend to use the Welsh language as a sort of code - works very well outside Wales - even inside sometimes. That's the connection you see - 'Megan' - scrawled on a wall near one of the victims...'

He suddenly looked at his watch and became more decisive! 'Right - well there you are then - when you are fully recovered I want you to take on this investigation - you'll be briefed, of course!' He stared at Rupert 'That is - I assume that you accept - don't you?' -

'Oh yes sir' said Rupert - before he could stop himself -

'Good chap! Splendid - knew you would! Well I must get on - take a few days leave Morgan - then to work eh?'

He strode to the door - nodding to Simon as he passed - Rupert sat upright and managed to blurt out -

'Just one thing sir?' the Chief turned -

'Yes?'

'Er - may I ask sir - why me? I mean I don't know much about electronics you know… '

There was something definitely furtive in the Chief's eyes - Rupert could swear there was -

'Ah' he turned - opened the door as if to make sure that his escape route was safe - 'well you see, Morgan, you are the only one who now has experience with em - - with - well with those types...

'What types?' Rupert almost shouted - but he knew the answer -

'Oh, didn't I tell you' said the Chief innocently - 'both the victims in Watford were gay!'

He vanished through the doorway before Rupert could even achieve one of his now classic gapes... Slowly he looked across at the Theatre Man called Simon - who just shrugged and smiled - Rupert let himself fall back onto the pillows - shut his eyes and wondered if there was such a garment as a chastity belt for men.

Finis.

Historical Note:

Darkly Flows the Taff *was written, and is set in 1986. Simon was working at Llandovery Theatre with young people, directing a youth film of The Taming of the Shrew, and writing scripts for the Company, until a few weeks before his death. He died from multiple cancers in October 2006, so his book is published posthumously.*

Waiting in the Wings!
The story and history of the love affair of his life, the 35 years dedicated to creative writing and performance, to building a theatre in the wild west of Wales - together with his wife Jacky - is the subject for the next story, now heading for publication.

What Country friends is this?
A theatrical Memoir of Simon Barnes and Jaqueline Harrison.